MYSTICAL BLYTHE COVE MANOR

A COLLECTION OF TALES

LORRAINE BARTLETT

A Dream Weekend, Copyright © 2015 by Lorraine Bartlett. All rights reserved.

A Final Gift, Copyright © 2016 by Lorraine Bartlett. All rights reserved.

An Unexpected Visitor, Copyright © 2016 by Lorraine Bartlett. All rights reserved.

Grape Expectations, Copyright © 2018 by Lorraine Bartlett. All rights reserved.

Foul Weather Friends, Copyright 2019 by Lorraine Bartlett. All rights reserved.

No part of this book may be reproduced in any form or by any electronic or mechanical means, including information storage and retrieval systems, without written permission from the author, except for the use of brief quotations in a book review.

Publisher's Note: The recipes contained in this ebook should be followed as written. The publisher is not responsible for any adverse reactions to the recipes contained in this ebook.

ALSO BY LORRAINE BARTLETT

THE VICTORIA SQUARE MYSTERIES

A Crafty Killing

The Walled Flower

One Hot Murder

Dead, Bath and Beyond (with Laurie Cass)

Yule Be Dead (with Gayle Leeson)

Murder, Ink (with Gayle Leeson)

Recipes To Die For: A Victoria Square Cookbook

LIFE ON VICTORIA SQUARE (*A companion series to the Victoria Square Mysteries*)

Carving Out A Path

A Basket Full of Bargains

The Broken Teacup

It's Tutu Much

The Reluctant Bride

THE LOTUS BAY MYSTERIES

Panty Raid (A Tori Cannon-Kathy Grant mini mystery)

With Baited Breath

Christmas At Swans Nest

A Reel Catch

Blythe Cove Manor

A Dream Weekend

A Final Gift

An Unexpected Visitor

Grape Expectations

Tales of Telenia (adventure-fantasy)

THRESHOLD

JOURNEY

TREACHERY

Short Stories

Love & Murder: A Bargain-Priced Collection of Short Stories

Happy Holidays? (A Collection of Christmas Stories)

An Unconditional Love

Love Heals

Blue Christmas

Prisoner of Love

We're So Sorry, Uncle Albert

For more information on Lorraine's books, check out her website:
http://www.LorraineBartlett.com

Other Books By Lorraine Bartlett

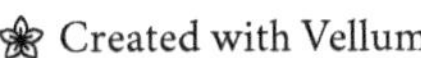 Created with Vellum

ABOUT BLYTHE COVE MANOR

Blythe Cove Manor is a beautiful bed and breakfast located on Martha's Vineyard, Massachusetts. It was the brainchild of three authors; Kelly McClymer, Shirley Hailstock, and myself, and based on the HGTV 2015 Dream Home. We felt it was the perfect place to tell the stories set in our (not so) imaginary B&B.

A Dream Weekend is the first of Lorraine's stories in this series.

Your hostess is owner/manager Blythe Calvert, and she's assisted by her tabby cat, Martha. There's always a little bit of magic at Blythe Cove.

Enjoy!

A DREAM WEEKEND

A TALE FROM BLYTHE COVE MANOR

DESCRIPTION

A DREAM WEEKEND

Serious life changes have pushed Paige and Alex Campbell to the brink of divorce. Still, they win a weekend at lovely Blythe Cove Manor and experience vivid dreams that take them back in time. Is there a chance this magical place inspires the nighttime fantasies that could help them fall in love again?

A DREAM WEEKEND

*I*t had not been just a quiet ride from Albany, New York to the ferry dock in Woods Hole, Massachusetts, but a silent one. Paige Campbell hadn't spoken a word to her husband of fifteen years, and he hadn't said a word to her, either. Paige turned on her e-reader as soon as they'd pulled out of the driveway of what now seemed like their enormous and empty home, and hadn't once let her gaze stray to the left side of the minivan where Alex sat behind the wheel.

The trip was nothing but an exercise in futility. The fact was they were headed for divorce, and a weekend stay in a high-end bed-and-breakfast in hoity-toity Martha's Vineyard wasn't going to eradicate the tragedy that had torn their lives apart.

The square white envelope arrived two weeks before. At first, Paige thought it was a wedding invitation, yet as she opened it she couldn't think of who among their family and friends might be heading for the state of holy matrimony. So she was surprised to find an engraved certificate for a free weekend at Blythe Cove Manor on Martha's Vineyard. Paige couldn't remember ever entering a sweepstake with that as a prize, and neither could

Alex. She'd quizzed their friends and family, but no one admitted to submitting their names for such a contest.

Paige called the inn and spoke with its owner, one Blythe Calvert, and was assured that, yes, she and her husband had indeed won the free weekend at the two hundred-year-old bed and breakfast.

Paige had checked out the website and if the photos didn't lie, Blythe Cove Manor was a lovely old inn that overlooked the eastern shore of the island. She'd studied the pictures of each of the rooms and hoped they'd be placed in one that overlooked the sea. Since they'd won some silly contest, it was more likely they'd be housed in the inn's worst accommodation. Considering the state of their marriage, Paige would not have complained if she and Alex were assigned a room with twin beds. It had been a long time since they'd been intimate. She never expected the two of them to make love ever again. Sex—maybe. Love? Never.

"Looks like we got here right on time," Alex said, interrupting her thoughts. His voice sounded rusty after so many hours without use, and yet Paige could detect a modicum of excitement there, too. Something she hadn't heard in a long time.

Paige looked up to see that the line of cars on the dock was already snaking into the multi-decked ferry. Should she allow herself to feel that same sense of excitement? That would be a betrayal and she couldn't bear the thought. What was the use anyway? The reality was, their lives were in ruins and nothing they could do or say would take back the worst year of their lives. Nothing could change what had happened. Nothing and no one could ever heal the wounds of loss they'd experienced.

"I've never been on a ferry before," Paige admitted and turned off her e-reader.

"Neither have I," Alex said and allowed the minivan to slowly roll forward.

When they got close to the boat, a workman held out his hand to collect the ferry pass that had accompanied the invitation to

Blythe Cove Manor. Whoever had supplied the prize seemed to have thought of everything.

Alex drove onboard and parked the van. He cut the engine and turned to Paige. "What do you want to do?"

"What do you mean?"

"You can either sit here and stew for the forty-five-minute ride to the island, or you can get out and go up on deck. I don't intend to sit here, but *you* can if you want."

Was that a challenge?

"It's a beautiful day. Why would I want to sit down here in the dark and stare at the horrible little car parked in front of us for the better part of an hour?"

Alex shrugged. He grabbed the Canon camera that sat on the floor between the bucket seats and opened the driver's side door. "Lock it up," he said, as if she needed that reminder.

Paige stowed her e-reader in the tote behind her seat, grabbed her purse, and followed the man she'd once vowed to love and cherish so long as they both shall live—a promise she no longer felt compelled to honor.

Alex hadn't waited for her and had forged ahead. Paige struggled to catch up to him, although she couldn't have said why. It's not like they valued each other's company. It's not like they conversed much these last few months. The love between them had evaporated and neither of them seemed inclined to try to resurrect it.

Paige trudged up the steel steps to the chilly open deck above. As she stepped into the bright sunlight, she was blinded for a few seconds. It was early in the season, just the first week in June, but those who were making the trip across the Vineyard Sound seemed as excited as though a holiday loomed. School hadn't yet let out for most of the northeast, which was probably the reason for the timing of the prize they'd won. Another couple of weekends and the inn—or was it a B&B?—would probably be booked solid until Labor Day. Still, there was nothing to keep Paige and

Alex at home during that a three-day, two-night stay. Not now, anyway.

No sooner had they walked toward the bow when the ferry left the dock, starting out at a slow pace, but soon picking up speed. The wind was brisk, and Paige was glad she'd gathered her hair into a ponytail that morning. She no longer felt the need to even attempt to look attractive. What did it matter in the grand scheme of things?

Alex settled his arms on the teak rail at the bow, his gaze focused on the vast expanse of blue sea before them. Paige did likewise, wondering how soon they'd be able to see the island.

"Why did you bring the camera?" Paige asked.

Alex's gaze was still fixed ahead of the big ferry. "I thought it might be time to make some new memories."

That was a laugh. Paige wanted to hold tight to her *old* memories. She wanted to go back in time to the lives they'd lived before their world had turned upside down. She wanted no part of the present or the future.

There, she'd actually allowed herself to think the dreaded thought that had been hovering at the edges of consciousness for the better part of a year. The sense of surprise she'd felt just seconds before quickly settled down to acceptance. Yes, perhaps she'd known right from the time the police had phoned what her inevitable choice would be. She glanced askance at Alex, whose face was filled with lines that hadn't been there a year before. The hair at his temples sported a bit of gray as well. Oddly enough, it suited him. It was the dead look in his eyes that often caught her off-guard, but then her expression mirrored his to the point that they might as well have been twins instead of husband and wife.

She wouldn't say another word about the camera. She'd let him make new memories, if that was what he wanted. And she decided she'd try to be nicer to him during the next few days. It would be her going-away present to him … one way or another.

ALEX CAMPBELL SNAPPED pictures of the ferry, its passengers and crew, and of the approaching island that seemed to glow in the afternoon sunlight as they approached. What he loved about digital photography was how easy it was to wipe away unsatisfactory shots with the press of a button. Of course, how many times had he cursed himself for wiping out so many mundane images the morning of the last day of his former life? But he'd made a point to clear the unwanted images away on a regular basis—just to keep the camera's memory uncluttered. Before that last day, he'd led a very orderly life. Since then, he'd let go of a lot of the internal clutter in his life. It had been far too many long months, but he was finally emerging from the mental fog that had engulfed him for too long.

He'd made a decision during the drive to Massachusetts. It was time to start living again.

The ferry approached the dock and he looked around for Paige, but didn't see her among the throng of people making a beeline for the stairs that led to the car decks. Perhaps she was already waiting for him in the van. He joined the line and trundled down the steps, but when he got to the van, he found the passenger seat empty.

The ferry docked and Alex had no choice; he had to move the vehicle. There were people parked behind it who would be irked to be held up from their weekend plans. Annoyed, he got in the van and started the engine. The cars ahead were already rolling forward and still, there was no sign of Paige. His irritation began to ebb, replaced by growing concern. Where the hell was she?

Putting the van in gear, he followed the car ahead and drove off the ferry, but pulled over at the first opportunity. Switching off the engine, he was about to get out of the vehicle when he glanced at the rearview mirror and saw a solitary figure disembark from the ferry, just as the vehicles heading back to the mainland began to fill the car decks once again.

It was Paige, of course.

Alex sat there, waiting, and finally, Paige walked up to the van, opened the passenger door, and got in.

"Sorry. I had to go to the bathroom and didn't know how long a time it would take to get to the inn, so I figured I'd better go while I had the chance," she said and buckled up.

"Better safe than sorry," Alex agreed, and then, impulsively, reached out to lay a hand on her arm. Paige pulled away. Well, what had he expected?

Alex started the van, shifted to drive, hit the accelerator, and the van rolled forward once again.

Alex was sure Paige no longer loved him, and some part of him couldn't blame her, but a bigger part was angry. That bigger part of his *soul* was just as angry at her. Angry that she'd written him off. Angry that she blamed him for something that was not his fault.

He wasn't sure he'd ever be able to forgive her for that.

BLYTHE CALVERT LOOKED up from her position behind the reception desk at the beautiful old inn the locals and visitors knew as Blythe Cove Manor. To her, it was simply home. The rambling old house had been in her family for more than two centuries—and sometimes it showed its age, like after a nor'easter hit and gripped the cedar shingles, wrenching them from the roof, or when one of the fireplaces would balk at digesting a load of wood. But most of the time, the house embraced her with a sense of safety and security, as it had taken care of generations of her family.

The sound of tires on gravel drew her attention, and Blythe peered through the storm door to see a blue minivan pull up in front of the house. She watched as the couple exited the vehicle, noticing the disconnect between the man and woman. They approached the house, but not as a unit. It seemed as though an invisible brick wall had been erected between them. They entered the lobby, looking around but not, Blythe noticed, at each other.

"Hello. Welcome to Blythe Cove Manor. I'm Blythe Calvert, your hostess. You must be Alex and Paige Campbell."

"We are," the wind-blown woman said and forced a smile that did not extend to her eyes. She crept closer to the reception desk. "We're not exactly sure what to do. We're the couple who won this weekend trip—"

"Yes. We've had a chilly few days, but it should warm up later this weekend. I do hope you'll enjoy yourself during your stay."

"Do you need a credit card to secure the room?" Mr. Campbell asked, even as he took in the antiques and bric-a-brac that decorated the eclectic lobby.

"No. As I explained to your wife when we spoke on the phone last week, everything has been taken care of."

"Even the tax and so forth?" Mrs. Campbell asked.

"Even that," Blythe assured them. She reached for a skeleton key that was attached to a scallop shell etched with the number six and handed it to Mrs. Campbell.

"Your room is down the hall to the left. We serve breakfast from six until nine o'clock. I can make a number of recommendations for dinner in town and would be happy to make the reservation, too. There's a notebook in your room with all the information you need to make a choice."

"Thank you," Mr. Campbell said. He turned to his wife. "Let's check out the room. We can bring in the rest of the luggage later."

Was that a hedge in case they didn't like the accommodations? Never mind. They'd be charmed—literally—about their room and everything else about Blythe Cove Manor.

The couple started off. "By the way," Blythe called. "You're not allergic to cats, are you?"

Mrs. Campbell turned. "No."

"Good. You'll probably see our resident tabby while you're here. Her name is Martha and she's as gentle as a lamb."

"Thanks for alerting us," Mr. Campbell said.

"There'll be sherry in the lobby this evening, and the luggage cart is just over there," Blythe said and pointed. "Let me know if you need anything."

Mr. Campbell nodded and turned away.

For a moment, the look on Mrs. Campbell's face changed from bland indifference to sheer panic. The poor dear needed something, but Blythe was sure no one on Earth could have given the woman what she so badly desired.

Mrs. Campbell swallowed and the mask of practiced detachment fell over her features once more. "Thank you."

Blythe watched them turn the corner and shook her head. This couple might prove to be a difficult one. Still, she had faith that Blythe Cove Manor would work its magic on them.

To save their marriage, it had to.

A PLAQUE GRACED the door to Blythe Cove Manor's room six. In gold-leaf calligraphy, it said: *Life holds a special magic for those who dare to dream.*

Paige handed the key over and allowed Alex to open the door. He stood aside to let her enter first. She took a step forward and paused in the doorway, a sudden smile tugging at the corners of her mouth. She had smiled so seldom during the past fifteen months that the muscles needed to achieve the expression seemed rusty from lack of use. But the room was so charming Paige couldn't help herself.

The walls were knotty pine, which could have made the space

feel dark and foreboding, but instead felt warm and cozy. The gas fire, which was alight, added to that ambiance. The queen-sized bed was covered in a faded patchwork quilt where a fat tabby—no doubt Martha—had taken up residence.

"Paige," Alex prodded.

"Oh. Sorry," she said, and moved deeper into the room so that he set down the one suitcase he'd brought in. Meanwhile, Paige found herself drawn to an old framed photograph that hung on the wall by the bed. It was a vintage wedding photo. The bride and groom wore clothing appropriate for the late 1880s. Perhaps they were the proprietress's ancestors. Maybe, Paige thought, she'd ask. At least it would give her something to say to the inn's owner the next time they met.

"The room looks nice," Alex said.

Paige didn't comment.

"I think I'll go get the rest of our stuff."

"Okay," Paige said without turning to look at him. She set her purse down on the bedside table as the door closed behind him and let out a breath. It was exhausting to be angry all the time, and when she was with Alex, she felt nothing but animosity. Or was it more betrayal? She was never quite sure.

Her fear of being stuck in inferior accommodations had been unfounded. The view through the sliding glass door that overlooked a small furnished patio was lovely. An expanse of green lawn seemed to lead to a bluff overlooking the ocean.

Paige turned away. Shrugging out of her sweater, she laid it across the pillow on her side of the bed and stepped over to the cat who hadn't moved, but had watched her every move.

Paige reached out to pet the feline, who immediately began to purr, and her thoughts traveled back to the long-winded debates she'd once participated in on why the Campbell family *needed* a pet. A rescue cat or dog—or even a guinea pig. They'd abruptly ended fifteen months before. As Paige petted the cat's soft fur, she wondered why she'd been so adamantly against the idea. After all, she'd grown up in a house with both cats *and* dogs.

Her arguments came back with a vengeance. Dogs smelled when they were wet. But when you were sad, they could be your best friend and confidant. Cats shed—even when you faithfully brushed them—leaving a trail of hair on rugs and furniture. The pleas for a pet had gone unheeded … another of Paige's regrets.

Martha stood and stretched.

"You can stay if you want," Paige offered, but the cat paid no attention to her invitation and jumped from the bed. It sauntered across the room and patiently settled before the door to the hall. Paige followed, opened it, and the cat swished its tail before taking its leave. "Come back soon," Paige said, actually meaning it.

Would spending time with the feline make up for times past?

No. Nothing would.

Alex returned with the luggage on a cart before she could shut the door and Paige moved deeper into the room.

"It's a nice room," he commented again as he unloaded their other suitcase, Paige's tote, and his camera bag. "It was thoughtful of Blythe to have the fire going for us."

"Yes," Paige agreed. "It sure has taken the chill off the day."

"I thought you asked for single beds?" he said.

"I did. I was told they only had full or queens. We got a queen."

"It's only for a few days," Alex said. "I'll be back in a few minutes."

He opened the door, struggling to get the luggage cart out and it was only after he left that Paige realized she should have helped him. The least they could offer each other was common courtesy.

She moved to stand before the fire. Years ago, she and Alex had once stayed in a B&B in Vermont. The fireplace had been wood burning and Alex couldn't get it to light—and he wouldn't let Paige call the inn's manager to help. She smiled. He'd wanted to do it all for her in those days. It had taken more than an hour before the kindling finally decided to burn, but he had given her a fire. This one could be turned on or off with the flip of a switch.

She liked a wood-burning fire better.

Alex returned and made a beeline for the leather club chair that sat in the corner. "It feels good to sit on something other than a car seat."

Paige said nothing as she looked around the room once more and saw there was no TV. Great. What were they supposed to do in the evenings—talk to one another? Make love? Fat chance of that happening.

There were no books, no magazines, not even a pamphlet to read.

"What time do you want to go to dinner?"

Alex shrugged. "Six?"

That gave them hours to kill.

"I wonder if we could find a bookstore. I forgot to load my e-reader and I've almost finished my current book."

"I guess."

That might kill an extra half hour, but that still left at least another ninety minutes to kill.

"I think I'll take a nap. Do you mind?"

"Go right ahead," Alex said.

Paige removed her sweater from the bed and hung it in the closet. She couldn't be bothered to unpack. Instead, she pulled back the quilt, carefully folded it and placed it on the bench at the bottom of the bed. Stepping out of her shoes, she climbed into the bed and lay on her side with her back to Alex.

Paige closed her eyes. She hadn't intended to actually sleep; she'd just wanted an excuse not to have to talk to Alex, but within moments she fell into a deep slumber.

ALEX DRUMMED his fingers on the arm of the chair. It helped to pass the time. He knew he should get up and go back to the lobby to ask their hostess where they could find a bookstore, but suddenly the tensions of the day seemed to weigh heavy on him. Maybe what he needed was forty winks. With nothing better to do, he got up.

"Paige?" No answer. That was no surprise. She was probably feigning sleep so she wouldn't have to actually talk to him. It certainly wasn't the first time. Well, she wouldn't have to do that much longer. He would wait until the ride home to bring up the subject of divorce. It could keep for another few days.

Alex yanked at the sleeves of his jacket, took it off, and tossed it on the chair. He kicked off his shoes and climbed onto the bed, making sure his back did not come anywhere near Paige's. The queen bed was a lot smaller than the king they shared at home. When they'd first moved in together, they'd slept in a double bed —a hand-me-down from a relative. Those were the good old days when all they could afford was a third-floor walk-up with a kitchen the size of the walk-in closet that now housed all Paige's clothes. His had been relegated to the guest room, not that he minded. What irritated him was being asked to leave their master suite. That was the beginning of the end.

The Windsor Complex near work had one- and two-bedroom apartments that looked elegant and probably cost a small fortune, but they came furnished and could be leased for as little as three months. That would give him time to figure out what he wanted to do and perhaps where to ultimately go. During the past decade, he'd turned down a couple of opportunities to relocate so that they could stay in the Albany area. They had reasons back then not to shake things up—not to disrupt their ordered lives. But then fate had intervened anyway and that way of life was gone forever.

Alex let out a breath and closed his eyes. In no time, sleep's oblivion claimed him, too.

It was raining on that blustery day in September at the State University at Buffalo's North Campus. Paige Abbott had pulled the hood of her poncho low over her eyes to keep her bangs dry and hadn't seen the soaked sophomore barreling toward her.

BAM! They collided—falling on their backsides into a puddle doing a good imitation of one of the Great Lakes.

"I'm so sorry," they said in unison.

They reached for each other's hands, pulling themselves up. Paige examined her sodden backpack and contemplated the condition of its contents; probably ruined. No chance to resell those books at the end of the semester. The guy standing in front of her seemed to have come to the same conclusion.

"I didn't see you," he said, hefting his dripping backpack over his left shoulder.

"Me, either."

"Let me apologize—inside—by buying you a cup of cocoa."

Cocoa? Not coffee? How did he know that was her preferred hot drink on a cold, miserable day?

"Ordinarily I'd say no, but—damn I'm cold."

"Then follow me."

The guy took Paige by the elbow and led her back up the steps and into the edifice. "I'm sorry there's no cafeteria in this building, but there are vending machines. The coffee sucks, but the hot chocolate is palatable."

Oh, so that's what he'd meant.

He led Paige down a series of corridors until they came to a bank of machines filled with beverages, candy, and chips. The guy scrounged in his pockets until he came up with enough change to buy two cups of steaming hot liquid. It was reminiscent of cocoa—but not nearly as good.

"Follow me," he said again and led her down another corridor where

a couple of heat registers were bolted to the wall clad in buff-colored ceramic tile.

"Sit down," he encouraged, and planted his damp butt on the heater. "We might be able to dry out a little before our next class."

"You must be missing one right now."

"You, too?"

"Yeah," she admitted.

"What's your program?"

"Social work."

"I'm in pre-law."

"What will your specialty be?"

"Anything but corporate law. That's my father's choice. He works for G.E."

"Must be good money."

"I won't have any student loans to replay—unless I piss off the old man, that is. How about you?"

"Student loans all the way. I'm mortgaging the next ten or fifteen years of my life, but I hope to make a difference in the lives of women and children."

"That's very noble of you," he said and sipped his chocolate.

Was he making fun of her? Maybe he wasn't such a nice guy after all.

Paige held the warm cup in her hands, hoping to absorb its heat. Only her bottom on the heater felt toasty.

"What's your name?"

"Paige Abbott."

"Alexander Greenfield Campbell, at your service," he said and offered her his hand. Paige shook it. Warm and strong—not that he'd crushed her fingers, but she suddenly got the impression this guy could do anything."

"Hi, Alexander."

"Call me Alex, Paige."

She smiled. "Okay."

"You from around here?"

She shook her head. "But not far. Dunkirk. How about you?"

"Schenectady."

"Will you be going home for Thanksgiving?"

He shook his head. My folks are heading for Florida, so there's no point."

"Do you have brothers or sisters?"

"One of each, but they're older than me. They have families of their own. How about you?"

"Two sisters. They both got married early. I'm the first one in my family who's going to graduate from college."

"Good for you. We're all trudging in my father's footsteps. Like my siblings, I'll be a third-generation lawyer."

"You don't sound thrilled."

He shrugged. "I'm not."

"What would you rather be?"

"An electrical engineer."

"So, change majors."

"And how do I pay for it?"

"The same as me."

He shook his head.

"Do you want to spend the rest of your life doing something you hate —or take the initiative—and also control of your life—and make your dreams come true?"

"Like it's that easy," he grumbled.

"Who said it was going to be easy?" She said with umbrage and sipped her chocolate. "I may be in hock, but I'll be doing something I want to do. They say if you love your job, you never have to work again. That's going to be me."

Paige drank the last of her chocolate. What a wuss, she thought, crumpling her empty cup, and just minutes before she thought he might be capable of just about anything. So much for woman's intuition.

She stood, didn't see a trash can nearby, and dropped the cup into her backpack. "It was nice meeting you, Alex."

"Hey, wait. Where are you going?"

"To the library to study."

"I've got another class. Maybe we could meet up later."

Paige shook her head. "I don't think so."

"Will you tell me why?" he asked, sounding sincere.

"My education means everything to me because I'm paying for it. I can't be distracted by people who aren't serious about their schoolwork, their lives, and their futures."

"That's a pretty heavy line to dump on a guy."

"Sorry." Paige forced a smile. "It was nice talking to you." Mostly. "Maybe we'll run into each other again some time, only next time—I hope not literally."

"Maybe," Alex said thoughtfully.

Paige gave a wave and headed back the way they'd come. She was almost to the exit when Alex caught up to her.

"Hey, wait!"

She turned to face him.

"I'm sorry. I must have come off as some kind of jerk. Please give me a second chance to prove myself."

Paige looked at him in confusion. "Why?"

"Because I sense that you're far different than anyone I've ever met before. I have this weird feeling that you might be the best thing that could ever happen to me."

Talk about a come-on line.

"But we've only just met."

Alex smiled and shrugged. "Maybe it's kismet."

Kismet? There was no such thing.

"And what if you're not the best thing to ever happen to me?" she asked.

His grin broadened. "Well, we'll never know if we don't get to know each other better. And I promise you, I may be conflicted about my future, but I'm determined to prove to you my worth."

Was this guy serious?

Something inside Paige softened. "Well, okay. What did you have in mind?"

"I don't have a lot of money, but I could afford to take you to dinner at a real restaurant—not just fast food. I know a place that has the best beef on weck sandwiches. The horseradish will clear your sinuses and may even extend your life."

"I do love kimmels," Paige admitted, referring to the caraway seeds on the buns.

"Then please give me a second chance."

Alex had the prettiest blue eyes. "Well, okay," she said.

His smile widened.

"PAIGE? WAKE UP, PAIGE."

Alex watched as his wife opened her eyes, blinking to focus on the heavy cotton golf shirt before her. Her gaze tilted upward to take in his face.

"You've slept for almost three hours. It's getting late. If we want to get some dinner, we need to get going."

Paige sat up and swung her legs off the bed. "What time is it?" she asked and rubbed her eyes.

"Just past seven. I would have woken you sooner, but I fell asleep, too."

Paige's stomach rumbled.

"See, you're as hungry as I am. I'm sure Ms. Calvert can give us a recommendation. How about seafood?"

"I guess." Still, she didn't seem in a hurry to get going.

Alex offered her his hand.

She looked at it for a long time before she raised her own and let him pull her to her feet. They stood together, too close, just staring at one another for a long moment, and Alex fought the urge to kiss her. He'd tried on other occasions and she'd turned from him. She didn't want comfort—she wanted to blame him for everything that had gone wrong. Still....

The moment passed and Paige dodged around him, heading for her suitcase. "My clothes are rumpled. I'd better change."

"You look fine. Just as pretty as the day we met."

Paige whirled around. "What did you say?"

Alex shrugged. "That you look as pretty as the day we met."

Paige just stood there, staring at him, her expression incredulous.

"What?" he asked at last, puzzled.

She shook her head and turned back for the suitcase. "Let me get my sweater, fix my face, and I'll be ready to go."

Alex watched as Paige headed for the bathroom and shut the door, then stared long afterward. Why had she looked at him so quizzically? Because he'd mentioned the first time they'd met? Funny, he hadn't thought of that day for a long, long time. The truth was he'd suppressed far too many such thoughts during the past fifteen months. Perhaps if he hadn't, things might be different between them.

He shrugged, turning away. They just had to get through the weekend. And who knew…maybe one day they might actually be more than just civil to one another.

THE LIGHTS WERE ablaze inside Blythe Cove Manor when they returned and Alex pulled the van to a halt in front of the inviting entrance. Not exactly like a Thomas Kinkade painting, but just as inviting. Alex cut the engine and Paige turned back to face him.

"Dinner was nice," she said. "I haven't had lobster in years."

"Me, either." He shook his head, a wry smile touching his lips. "For a lot of years, we couldn't *afford* lobster."

Paige caught herself before she, too, smiled, by averting her gaze. Suddenly it felt awkward to be together … sort of like a couple who'd gone out on a first date. In fact, that was how the evening had gone. A stroll down the street to the restaurant—

although they didn't hold hands—and then they'd been seated by a window that overlooked the sea. They'd watched the sky darken and the clouds take on a lovely peach-colored huge before the sea engulfed the last light of day and the moon shone on the rippling water. And their conversation had been light, not tense like it had been for more than a year. She didn't want to think about those dark times.

"I guess we should go in. Didn't Blythe say something about sherry?"

"Yes, she did."

"Why don't you move the car and I'll look for it and pour us a couple of glasses."

"Sounds good to me."

Paige nodded and got out of the car, while Alex restarted the engine. She paused for a moment to listen to the tires crunch the gravel before entering the lobby. The reception desk was empty, with no sign of the other guests or their hostess, but as promised a decorative crystal carafe of sherry and two delicately etched glasses stood on a silver tray, as though awaiting them.

Paige settled onto the big leather couch, uncapped the bottle and poured. She'd just finished the task when Alex arrived. He took off his light jacket before taking the chair to her right. A flash of disappointment coursed through her. For a moment she'd thought he might actually perch next to her, but then he was probably afraid to do so—in case his actions spoiled the unspoken truce they seemed to have called.

Paige picked up her glass. It felt like she should offer a toast, but she didn't want to do that and hoped Alex would resist the temptation as well.

He did, picking up his glass and taking a sip. "Not bad." He studied his glass.

Paige sank further back into the couch and sipped her sherry. Maybe she *should* have offered a toast. And what would it have been? To happier times?

Suddenly Alex hoisted his glass, looking straight for her. "To happier times."

Paige blinked. "What did you say?"

"To happier times. For both of us." He scrutinized her face. "Why do you have such an odd expression?"

Paige shook her head, rather disconcerted. "It's just that … I was thinking the same thing." She just hadn't been about to voice it.

Alex shrugged. "It's nice to know we still have the same mindset on *something*."

Paige bit her lip to keep from commenting. She didn't want to spoil what had been the most pleasant evening she'd had in a very long time. And yet, at the same time, she wondered why. Earlier in the day, she'd made up her mind to end the terrible existence that had been her life, but now doubt began to creep in.

Paige looked over at her husband. When they married, she thought it was forever. Her forever, however, would come to an end at fifteen years. Alex smiled. True, it bore little resemblance to his smiles of the past—perhaps more wistful—but it was a smile.

This time, Paige managed to give him the shadow of one in return.

Alex was the first to get ready for bed that night. He'd bought a guide to Martha's Vineyard at the bookstore, and had made a considerable a dent in it when Paige finally changed into a night-gown and crawled into bed.

"I'll turn the light off," Alex said.

"You don't have to," she said diffidently. "It doesn't bother me. I thought I might watch the fire until I feel drowsy enough to fall asleep."

"It's nice having a fireplace in the bedroom." He wanted to say romantic, but he didn't want to put a damper on what had been the best evening they'd shared in a very long time.

"I suppose it'll be too warm for a fire in another week or so. I wonder what the inn looks like at Christmastime."

We could visit and see, Alex thought about saying, but decided against it. He was supposed to be signing a lease for one of the Windsor Complex's apartments next week. They would have to talk about what to do with the house. He didn't think Paige would want to live there all alone—not with all the memories they'd made there. The Christmases, birthdays, hot summer nights spent stargazing—while slapping mosquitoes—and all the other wonderful celebrations. It was a shame all those memories had to be shelved. And what would they do with all the furniture, bric-a-brac, and photographs? Splitting the photos would be the hardest. Then again, he could just scan them all and let her keep the prints. There always seemed to be a sanitary solution to most of their problems ... if they cared to go to the trouble.

Alex set his book aside and switched off the bedside lamp. The gas flames from the fireplace threw leaping shadows around the walls.

"It's pretty, isn't it?" Paige asked quietly.

"Yes. Very pretty."

They didn't say any more.

Alex watched the shadows for a while before closing his eyes, then instantly fell asleep.

A woman's wedding day was supposed to be the happiest day of her life, but as Paige's wedding day approached everything seemed to go wrong. It started when the RSVP cards began to arrive.

Alex's parents decided not to come due to a prior engagement. And what kind of engagement would keep you from your son's wedding?

They'd never forgiven him for changing his major, and not coming to the wedding was their way of punishing him.

Alex's brother Ron, and his wife, Amy, and kids had vacation plans that couldn't be changed. Funny, he hadn't mentioned those plans when Alex had spoken to him six months before when the "save the date" cards had gone out.

Alex's sister, Joanne, at least had a reasonable excuse. At eight months pregnant with her second child, her obstetrician had given her a "no travel" edict.

And Paige's family had let her down as well. Her sister, Emily, had called to say her car had died and that she and her husband couldn't afford to rent one to drive to Buffalo—nor could she find a friend willing to drive them.

So it was with a feeling of doom that Paige had donned her ivory tea-length wedding dress on that sultry summer morning. It was the "something old" part of the day, as she'd found it for a great price at a thrift shop along Buffalo's Main Street. Something blue? A garter she'd bought. Something new? The floral headpiece and short veil she'd made herself.

As the hour for the nuptials approached, Paige grew more and more apprehensive as her best friend from childhood had not yet arrived.

"It's okay, Paige," her sister, Lisa, said, her voice a calming balm. "If worse comes to worst, I can stand in."

"Oh, thank you," Paige said, giving Lisa a hug.

When the organist struck the first few notes of Wagner's Wedding March, Lisa grabbed the Maid of Honor's bouquet and marched down the aisle as though she had been the bride's first choice of attendant.

Alex stood at the end of the chapel's aisle, but the man standing next to him was not the guy he had asked to stand up for him, but another buddy who hadn't even worn a suit. Paige missed a step, wondering if this marriage had been cursed because so many of their friends and family were missing from the celebration.

But then she locked eyes with Alex, and took in the broad grin he sported. And she smiled, too. What did it matter if some of the invitees were absent? All that really counted was the fact that she loved Alex, and he loved her, and from that day forward they were to be as one.

Paige walked slowly, step-by-step, alone. She had no father or father figure to give her away. And it was with shyness that she paused before her betrothed. She handed Lisa her bouquet, and Alex gently took her hands in his, beaming; a smile that could have lit the continent. Then the two of them turned their gazes to the minister who stood a step higher than them.

"Paige and Alex, welcome to the beginning of your new life together."

Paige couldn't really process everything the minister said. She felt overwhelmed, but happier than she'd ever been. She was about to commit the rest of her life to the man who completed her, and felt sure that she, too, would complete him.

Lisa gave her sister a nudge, handing her a simple gold band.

The minister spoke. "Paige, place the ring on Alex's finger and repeat after me: With this ring."

Paige looked directly into Alex's blue eyes. "With this ring."

"I pledge my love and faithfulness to you."

"I pledge my love and faithfulness to you."

"Today, tomorrow and always."

"Today, tomorrow and always." Paige slipped the ring on Alex's finger, giving him a shy smile.

The minister directed his attention to the groom. "Alex, place the ring on Paige's finger and repeat after me: With this ring."

It was Alex's turn to gaze into Paige's eyes. "With this ring."

"I pledge my love and faithfulness to you."

"I pledge my love and faithfulness to you."

"Today, tomorrow and always."

"Today, tomorrow and always, always, always."

The minister smiled. "Then by the powers vested in me by the State of New York, I now pronounce you husband and wife. Alex, you may kiss your bride."

They leaned close and Alex brushed a gentle kiss against Paige's lips. Then another—with more intensity and the promise of more to come.

Then the organist launched into Mendelssohn's Wedding March. Lisa handed Paige her bouquet and the happy couple charged up the aisle.

And it was, after all, the happiest day of Paige's life....

So far.

BREAKFAST AT BLYTHE COVE MANOR was truly a delight—at least Blythe Calvert always thought so. She carefully planned her menus, baked sinful treats in her cream-colored AGA stove, and always tried to set a lovely table.

It was nearly nine and she was about to pack up the muffins, croissants, and strudel that sat on multi-tiered plates in her breakfast room when the Campbells finally came down for their morning repast.

"Are we too late?" Mr. Campbell asked.

"Not at all."

"It's just that we slept so well last night. Better than we have in such a long time," Mrs. Campbell practically gushed. She certainly looked better rested than she had when they'd arrived the previous day.

"I'm always glad to hear that," Blythe said. "Can I get you some coffee?"

"Yes, please."

"Take a seat wherever you'd like," she said, and headed back to the kitchen to get the fresh pot. When she returned to the breakfast room, she found the Campbells had chosen the coveted table that overlooked the sea.

"Seems like we're the last for breakfast."

"It's not a problem," Blythe said as she poured the brew. "What are your plans for today?"

Mr. Campbell brandished a guide book. "We thought we might like to visit the Edgartown Lighthouse."

"And maybe the cottages at Oak Bluffs," Mrs. Campbell said with what sounded like hope in her voice. Her eyes were still shadowed, and her voice tentative, but she seemed to have relaxed some in the eighteen-or-so hours since their arrival.

"Oh, you'll love them. They're adorable."

"We were wondering," Mr. Campbell began, "how it is that we won a weekend at your beautiful inn. Neither of us remembers entering our names in any contests."

"The contest was held through Vineyard Vines magazine. Perhaps one of your friends or relatives entered your names."

Mr. Campbell frowned, as though that wasn't a viable answer.

"What can I get you for breakfast? Blueberry pancakes? Sausage? Bacon?"

"Pancakes sound wonderful," Mrs. Campbell said. "With sausage?" She looked as though she had lost weight and could use a good solid meal.

"And you?" Blythe asked Mr. Campbell.

"The same, please."

She nodded. "Feel free to help yourselves to anything on the buffet across the way. I'll be back with your breakfasts in a few minutes."

While the pancakes sizzled on the grill, Blythe snuck a peek into the breakfast room to see the Campbell's quietly contemplating the guide book. They were talking. That was a good sign. She had the feeling they hadn't had much to discuss for quite some time.

She plated the pancakes and sausage, placing a sprig of curly parsley from her kitchen garden, and brought them into the breakfast room, snagging a pitcher of maple syrup on the way. "Here you go," she said, sliding each plate in front of her guests. "If there's anything you need, please don't hesitate to ask. I'll be in the kitchen."

"Thank you," they chorused.

Humming Beethoven's "Ode to Joy," Blythe returned to the

kitchen and the mountain of dishes that sat in the big porcelain farm sink. Some days she just loaded the dishwasher, but other days she enjoyed washing the plates, cups, and cutlery by hand. It was such a beautiful day, and the magic of Martha's Vineyard was practically palpable, so she put the stopper in the sink, turned on the hot tap, and watched as the water rose and the bubbles morphed.

It would be a very good day indeed for the Campbells—and for her, too

THE DAY WAS one to remember. Sunny skies, balmy breezes, and lovely vistas. Alex snapped picture after picture and realized it had been a long, long time since he had experienced real pleasure. The lighthouse had been a delight. Paige had been enchanted by the charming cottages at Oak Bluffs, which were painted in pastel shades, looking like doll houses brought to life for their full-sized occupants. She'd not only smiled, but directed him to take photos of them all. For the first time in a long time, she had shown an interest in something. That she was interested in anything seemed like a hopeful sign that she might be moving beyond depression and utter hopelessness.

Lunch had been a relaxed affair of lobster rolls and chardonnay. They hadn't talked much, but there weren't any awkward—angry—silences, either.

They'd finished the day with a leisurely dinner at the island's most famous restaurant, after which they'd walked the two blocks to reclaim their minivan and this time when Alex reached for Paige's hand, she'd curled her fingers around his. All too soon, they reached the van and separated. He'd unlocked the passenger side door and she'd climbed aboard.

Like most of the rest of the day, the ride back to Blythe Cove Manor was quiet.

"Do you want to stop by the lobby for sherry?" Alex asked as they turned down the lane that led back to Blythe Cove manor.

Paige sighed. "I don't think so. Unless you do."

"No. I just thought I'd ask."

"It was a long day. The best day I've had in … a long time."

"Me, too."

"I feel guilty," Paige said, her voice sounding small.

"You shouldn't."

"I know, but I can't help it."

They didn't speak again until they pulled into the inn's lot. Alex parked the van and they got out, their shoes crunching on the gravel. They wiped their feet before entering the spotless lobby. Like the night before, they didn't see any of the other guests, who must have all retreated to their rooms.

"You know, I haven't seen anyone else here this weekend," Paige commented

"There are other cars in the lot," Alex pointed out.

"I know, but it just seems rather odd."

"Well, we aren't exactly the most sociable people these days, so…." He let the sentence trail off. They'd lost touch with just about all their friends and family. People whose company they had enjoyed. People he knew that cared. It was just too awkward to be around them and their families.

"That's true," Paige admitted as they reached their room.

Alex unlocked the door, reached in to turn on the light, and then let Paige enter.

"I'm going to bed early," she announced.

"I think I'll do the same."

She nodded and opened the dresser drawer, pulling out her nightgown and headed for the bathroom. There was a time when she would undress in front of Alex, but now modesty seemed to have taken over. She'd been like that for too long. She was still an attractive woman—or could be—even though she no longer put any effort into it.

Alex sat in the chair and removed his shoes. He really wasn't ready for sleep. He could reread the guidebook, but he didn't feel like it. If only they could talk. They used to be able to talk about anything. He missed his former confidant. He missed their old life. Since they'd arrived at the inn, she'd been different. Perhaps they'd both been different. Still, he had no illusions that the break from animosity and hurt wouldn't last any longer than the drive home, and for that he felt sorry.

He missed the woman he'd loved and married.

It all started with a phone call.

Alex and Chrissy, their twelve-year-old daughter, had gone to the grocery store for a gallon of milk and a sack of potatoes several hours before. It wasn't all that unusual that what should have taken fifteen minutes had lengthened into hours. Chrissy had discovered maps at the tender age of four and had been fascinated ever since.

She'd first mapped their home, then their yard, then the street. Alex would drive her around the area as Chrissy took notes on new streets to add to her drawings and penciled database. By age thirteen, she'd reached out to local government and private cartographers. She used Google Street View and the computer's mouse to drive the streets of Albany and the highways of China and beyond. She was happy because at such an early age she knew what her life's work was to be.

And it all unraveled when the phone rang late on that rainy Saturday afternoon in March.

"Mrs. Campbell?"

"Yes," Paige answered cautiously.

"This is Sergeant Mark Evans of the Colonie Police Department."

Paige's heart skipped a beat. "What happened?" she asked, dreading the answer.

"There's been an accident."

Paige swallowed, her mouth going dry. "How bad?"

"Pretty bad, ma'am. Your husband and daughter have been taken to the Albany Medical Center."

"And?"

"Witnesses said an SUV ran the red light and T-boned your husband's car."

"And?"

"I'm sorry, but I don't have any other information."

"Thank you. I'll—I'll go there right now."

"Good luck, ma'am."

Paige hung up the phone and looked around their orderly home. A batch of towels tumbled in the dryer and she wondered if she ought to fold them and put them away before—

Then she caught herself. What in God's name was she thinking when Alex and Chrissy were hurt—and badly, too, if she'd understood what the officer's tone conveyed.

Paige grabbed her coat and purse and headed out the door.

The gray sky was beginning to darken on that first day of spring as Paige drove a little too fast to the hospital, hoping she wouldn't grab the attention of a traffic cop. She parked and practically ran toward the Emergency Room, bursting through the automatic doors into the ER's lobby. A line snaked in front of the receptionist's desk and she was sure she would jump out of her skin during the five-minute wait for her turn.

"My husband and daughter were in a car accident. The police called me."

"Name?"

"Campbell. My husband's name is Alexander. My daughter is Christina."

The receptionist's eyes darted back to her computer screen. "Mr. Campbell is in unit three."

"And my daughter?"

The receptionist glanced at her screen again. "You need to speak to Dr. Sharma. I'll put in a call."

Panic filled every molecule of Paige's body. Why wasn't Chrissy assigned an emergency cubicle—they'd been brought in together?

"Please follow me," the receptionist said, raised the counter on hinges that kept those in the lobby at bay, and led Paige to a small room. "Dr. Sharma will be right with you." She gave a half-hearted smile, left the room, and closed the door.

The cell-like room was no more than five steps across. Painted a soft blue, it contained a loveseat and a couple of chairs. The prints on the wall were of pansies. Summer flowers.

Paige couldn't stand to sit and paced the room. She knew—she already knew what this Dr. Sharma was going to say, but she wouldn't believe it. She couldn't believe the worst. Not until she saw for herself, until she could touch—kiss—her sweet baby girl. Still, she made no move to leave the room.

Paige only had time to pace three or four circuits before the handle rattled and the door opened. A young dark-skinned man entered.

"Mrs. Campbell?" he asked, with only the hint of an accent. "I'm Dr. Sharma, the resident on duty. Won't you please sit?" he said, indicating the loveseat.

Paige sat, holding the straps of her purse in a death grip. "She's gone, isn't she?" she asked, her voice sounding stronger than her spirit.

Sharma nodded sadly. "Your daughter was alive when they brought her in, but she sustained massive blood loss. Her injuries were too great for us to help her."

"Did she suffer?" Paige asked, her voice shaky.

Sharma shook his head. "I'm so sorry for your loss."

Paige swallowed hard and nodded, determined not to give into the emotions she held back by a dam of resolve. "And my husband?"

"Mr. Campbell suffered a broken collar bone, a fractured tibia, as well as multiple contusions. He should recover without lasting after-effects."

"Does he know about our daughter?"

Sharma shook his head.

Again, Paige nodded. She was beginning to feel like a bobblehead. "Can I see Chrissy?"

"I would advise you not to at this time," Sharma said firmly.

What did that mean? Were her injuries so horrific that seeing them might scar Paige for the rest of her life? Did she really want to see her perfect child in that condition or remember her beautiful face as she was?

Good Lord—was this really happening? How could this happen to her—to her family?

"However," Sharma continued, "your husband is conscious. He has asked for you several times."

Again Paige swallowed hard. She let out a long, unsteady breath. "Okay." She rose to her feet.

Sharma opened the door and she followed him to a curtained unit. He paused. "Please let any of our staff know if you or Mr. Campbell needs anything," he said kindly.

"Thank you."

He gave her a sad smile, and left her.

Paige let out another long breath, steeling herself before she faced Alex ... before she had to shatter his world like hers had been shattered.

Pulling the curtain aside, Paige entered the cubicle. Alex lay propped up in the hospital bed, covered in white blankets, with an IV bag hanging above him and a heart monitor beeping quietly—reassuringly —behind him. His eyes were closed—his face bruised, brush-burned, and swollen. Her heart lurched and she had to swallow several times before she could make herself step forward. She reached over the bed rail and clasped Alex's hand in her own. His skin felt cold to the touch, but he was alive, she reminded herself, and rubbed her thumb over the top of his hand.

Alex's eyes fluttered open. "Paige?"

"I'm here," she said, her voice not much above a whisper.

"Chrissy. What happened to Chrissy?" he asked frantically. "Nobody will talk to me."

"Tell me what happened," Paige said, her words calm—patient—not what she was feeling at all.

Alex seemed to deflate. "We'd taken a detour. Chrissy wanted to see the new housing development near the mall. She wanted me to drive through the streets so she could get an idea of the layout. I told her we should wait until they update the aerial view from Google Maps, but you know Chrissy. She whined and looked at me with those big blue eyes and the next thing I knew we were driving up and down muddy tracks while she made notes."

Just as Paige had suspected.

"And then?"

"We were heading home. We got the green light when suddenly this big black SUV came barreling through the intersection and hit us. That's all I remember until I woke up here a little while ago. Have you seen Chrissy?" he asked, his voice rising.

"No," Paige managed. "I haven't seen her."

"Is she okay?"

"No, she's not." Could she be more blunt? Maybe she should wait to tell Alex. Was he going to require surgery for that broken leg? She didn't even know.

"We've never kept secrets, Paige," Alex reminded her.

Again, Paige swallowed and bit her lip. "No, we never have." She let out a long breath. "They tell me ... they tell me she's gone."

"Gone?" Alex asked, disbelief coloring his tone.

Paige nodded, grinding her teeth so that she wouldn't break down.

"She—she can't ...." But Alex didn't seem able to complete the sentence. His eyes squeezed shut and he began to tremble. Paige moved closer, until his head sagged against her and he began to cry—great heaving sobs. She'd only ever seen Alex cry one other time—in the delivery room when Chrissy was born. They'd both cried tears of joy, but now she seemed incapable of tears. All she could do was hold onto Alex and try to comfort him ... because she knew that Chrissy's death was something she would never, ever get over.

And she vowed that she would never, ever cry. She was too angry to cry. Angry at the stupid driver of the SUV. Angry at fate. Angry at a God who would let that beautiful child with so much potential, such a beautiful spirit, to be taken from them.

At that moment, Paige was forever changed. A coldness surrounded her heart. An icy prison so formidable that nothing could penetrate it. Not sorrow, not joy … not even love.

That was it. She would never allow herself to love anyone ever again.

Not.

Ever.

ALEX AWOKE to the sound of muffled sobs, the bed shaking in the dark.

"Paige?" he called groggily, and reached across the expanse of mattress to gently touch her shoulder. He expected her to pull away, as she had so many times during the last year, but this time she rolled toward him, burying her face in his shoulder.

"I don't want to die," Paige wailed and started to cry even harder.

"Hey, hey," Alex soothed, wrapped his arms around his wife and kissed her forehead. "You're not dying."

"But I'd planned … after we got home … after you left me."

Her words were like a knife in his soul.

"Oh, Paige," Alex said sadly, but he couldn't admit that that had indeed been his plan.

"I was angry with you because…." A sob kept Paige from continuing.

"Because I lived and she didn't?"

She nodded. "At first I was glad I still had at least one of you, but as the months went by…."

She didn't have to say it. Every day Alex questioned why he'd been spared but his daughter had died. Because the SUV that had crashed into them had hit the passenger side when running the light. Alex had never even seen it coming. Survivor's guilt ate at him and it had taken more than a year for him to come to terms with the reality that fate had spared him. Perhaps there was a reason. To save Paige from the horrible depths of her grief.

"Chrissy's dead!" Paige wailed. "She's dead and I'll *never* get over it. I'll *never* be happy again."

"You're right," he soothed, his voice ragged with emotion he's tried for so long to stifle. "You will never get over Chrissy's loss. Neither of us will. Neither will anyone who ever knew that golden girl. But you *can* be happy again. We can *both* be happy again, but only if we remember why we got together in the first place. Why we got married. Why we vowed to be together today, tomorrow, and always, always, always."

Her sobs quieted and he could just see the glint of her damp eyes in the room's scant light. "You remembered," she said, her voice sounding small and subdued.

Alex smoothed her hair back away from her face. "You silly girl, I never forgot."

And then they were hugging one another with an intensity they hadn't mustered for many, many years. They kissed, and kissed again, and Alex was overcome with such a feeling of desire —of protection—for this beautiful, now fragile woman who'd taken herself out of his life—had given up *on* life. Was there a chance they could make it work once again?

If he did nothing else for the rest of his life, Alex knew he had to do everything in his power to try.

THE DRIVE back to Albany was quiet, but this time the atmosphere inside the van was devoid of tension and replaced with a sense of love, and finally ... understanding. They'd made a joint decision to do everything they could to repair their shattered marriage.

Alex steered the van up the driveway of their house in Albany and cut the engine. "Home again, home again—"

"Jiggity-jig." Paige finished the phrase without thinking. It had been something they'd said—and shared with their daughter—upon arriving home ever since Chrissy was a toddler. For a moment Paige thought she might cry, but then she managed a wan smile. Chrissy had loved the ritual. Just because she was gone didn't mean they should abandon such rites. In fact, Paige felt determined to remember the best of their times with Chrissy, to honor them, instead of trying to eliminate all memory of them.

She cleared her throat. "I was thinking that since we had such a big breakfast that we might want to have a light supper."

"Do we have anything in the fridge?"

"Everything we need to make waffles."

Chrissy had loved waffles, and neither of them had eaten them since the day they'd lost their daughter. They hadn't eaten any of her favorite foods. They hadn't celebrated any occasions. They had mourned and forgotten how to live. It was time to start over. To finally heal.

"I think I'd like that."

Again Paige smiled. "Me, too."

THE SKY WAS gray and a cold wind blew off the ocean on a cold late afternoon in April a year later. Blythe walked the length of the B&B's driveway to collect the day's mail. When she got back inside she thought she might make a nice apple crisp for dessert. The spicy smell would fill the kitchen and it would make a nice treat for her guests if they came back from dinner with just a little room left in their stomachs.

The mailbox was filled with circulars, bills, and a small white envelope. She smiled at seeing the return address in the upper left-hand corner but had decided to wait until she came back inside to the warmth of the inn to open it.

After hanging up her coat, she sorted through the mail,

discarding the junk which would go to the recycle box, and setting the bills aside. Blythe headed for the inn's reception area, which often doubled as her personal desk Picking up a brass letter opener, she slit the small white envelope, removing its contents. Little yellow ducks swam across the blue background on the bottom of the delightful picture announcement.

Rub-a-dub-dub,
there's a new baby
in the tub!
Ian Christopher Campbell
was born on
March 20th
7lbs 3oz ~ 20½ inches
to proud
Parents
Alex & Paige

Blythe's heart nearly melted as she studied the baby's delighted smile. He looked like his daddy, but had his mommy's eyes.

Martha strolled into the room. *"M'row!"*

Blythe looked up from the photo.

"What?"

"M'row!" Martha insisted, and walked in a circle.

"You want me to follow you?"

"M'row!"

"Oh, all right." Blythe set the announcement down as the cat disappeared around the corner. She came out from behind the desk, and trailed after the feline. Martha sat in front of room six, her tail swishing. She mewed again. "What do you want to go in there for?" Blythe asked.

"M'row!" Martha insisted.

"Oh, all right," Blythe said, taking out her master key. She unlocked the door and the cat marched in ahead of her, immediately jumping onto the bed.

Blythe had always loved this room and had enjoyed decorating it. But what always caught her attention was the vintage framed photo on the wall. This time she noticed it more because it was crooked. She crossed the room in seven steps and adjusted the ornate oval frame and smiled. It was uncanny how the couple in the sepia photo so strongly resembled one of the room's former occupants.

None other than Alex and Paige Campbell.

IF YOU ENJOYED...

If you enjoyed *A Dream Weekend* please consider spreading the word and reviewing it on your favorite online review site. Thank you!

A FINAL GIFT

A TALE FROM BLYTHE MANOR

DESCRIPTION

A FINAL GIFT

Will anything heal the pain of a grieving daughter? When a trip meant to be a gift of a weekend trip together turns into a painful solo journey, can the magic of Blythe Cove Manor help heal Jenny Taylor's soul?

CHAPTER 1

*J*enny Taylor accepted the keys to her rental car, grabbed hold of the handle of her rolling suitcase, and headed for the parking lot, unable to let go of the melancholy that gripped her soul. The dull gray sky did nothing to buoy her spirits. For some reason, she'd expected sunny skies and balmy breezes to greet her when she and her mother planned the trip some six months before.

"Can you imagine a prettier place to be?" she'd asked.

Truthfully, Jenny really hadn't known what to expect. Oh, she'd heard about Martha's Vineyard and had probably seen pictures of celebrities—like actors and politicians—who'd chosen the island four miles from the Massachusetts mainland as a place to get away from it all, but it was really her mother, Caroline, who'd longed to visit the isle. She had planned—and paid—for the trip, or at least the accommodations.

Jenny's first inclination had been to cancel the journey, but it was her best friend, Missy, who'd convinced her to carry on with her plans. "It's what your Mom would have wanted," she'd insisted.

Yes, she would have, Jenny thought. "The room has double beds —come along with me."

"I'd love to," Missy said, "but I've got a wedding to go to that weekend. Bess was my best friend back in grade school. I've already sent in the RSVP."

Nobody else Jenny knew was free that early weekend in May, either. She'd have to make the trip alone, which promised to be a bust. Still, with Missy otherwise occupied, and no men currently in her life, Jenny carried on with the plans.

Unlocking the car, she stowed the suitcase in the back and climbed into the driver's seat. She put the key in the ignition but didn't start it. Instead, she removed from her purse the buff-colored envelope with the embossed scallop shell on the back flap and took out the typewritten letter from the proprietress of the bed and breakfast where she was to stay, Blythe Cove Manor.

The name sounded opulent, but she'd checked the inn's website and found it to be a charming, rather rambling, two-story property over two hundred years old. She and her mother had been booked into the Calvert Cottage that overlooked the back garden, but Jenny hoped she could change rooms upon checking in. The thought of seeing the unused bed was sure to further dampen her spirits.

The B&B's owner, a Ms. Calvert, had mailed a map with instructions on how to find the manor, and Jenny reviewed them once again before setting them down on the passenger side seat. She clasped the charm that hung from a silver chain around her neck. "Ready for adventure, Mom?"

Nobody answered, and Jenny fought the urge to cry. That wasn't what her mother would have wanted. She let go, cleared her throat, and started the car. The radio immediately blasted Kelly Clarkson belting out lyrics that seemed to resonate with Jenny. *What doesn't kill you makes you stronger.*

Right then, Jenny felt anything but strong. Still, she moved the gearshift to drive, took her foot off the brake, and drove out of the lot.

For better or for worse, she was committed to staying the weekend on Martha's Vineyard and was determined to make the best of it. She wouldn't let sadness overtake her. Caroline meant for the weekend to be a happy one—a mother-daughter celebration.

How sad that Jenny would have to spend it alone.

She shook herself, feeling tired from the flight from Ohio and then the hassle of getting to the ferry dock and the chilly ride across Vineyard Sound. Perhaps she should find somewhere to eat first. According to the inn's website, only breakfast was served. Yes, maybe she'd splurge for lobster fresh from the sea. It was the thought of eating alone in some homey restaurant that made her feel alone—all alone—in this great big world.

CHAPTER 2

The shadows had already begun to lengthen and Blythe Calvert strained to look across the lobby and out the front door's beveled glass to see if her final guest for the weekend had arrived. Technically, check-in was between three and six o'clock, but it was already past seven and there was no sign of the mother-daughter duo meant for the Calvert Cottage.

"*Brrrpt!* Martha, the B&B's resident tabby trilled from under the heat of a Tiffany lamp that sat on one of the end tables.

"You know you're not supposed to sit there," Blythe chided. The cat merely closed her eyes as if to say, "So what?"

Blythe shook her head and checked over the recipe for the cake she intended to bake the next morning. Did she have a can of crushed pineapple? She'd have to check the pantry. Preparations for the afternoon tea were well underway. Her collection of bone china teacups had been washed; she'd chosen the serving dishes and had finalized the menu just the day before. Even if the heavens opened up—which, unfortunately, was the forecast— Blythe Cove Manor would be snug and warm. She'd light a fire and the manor's cozy atmosphere would enchant its roster of guests.

Now she just had to hope her final guests would actually arrive.

She needn't have worried. Despite the lobby door being closed to keep out the chill, she heard the muffled crunch of tires on the gravel drive. A car pulled up outside the door and a pretty young woman in her mid-twenties exited the vehicle, removed a suitcase from the back, and turned for the door. She entered the lobby.

"Welcome to Blythe Cove Manor," Blythe called as the woman approached. She looked expectantly beyond her solitary guest. "Are you Jenny Taylor?"

"Yes."

Again, Blythe looked through the door, but there didn't appear to be anyone else in the car.

"And will Caroline be joining you?"

Jenny shook her head. "I'm afraid it's just me."

Blythe wasn't sure how to reply.

"This was supposed to be for a weekend vacation for my mother and me. Unfortunately, she passed away not long ago."

"Oh, I'm so sorry. Had she been ill?" Blythe asked.

"No, and that's the shocking thing. An aneurysm. There was no warning." Jenny sighed, looking like she might burst into tears. Then she straightened. "But my friends urged me not to cancel the reservation and to make the trip to Martha's Vineyard anyway." She forced a cheerless smile. "So far, so good."

"But lonely?" Blythe guessed.

"Sad," Jenny corrected.

Blythe noticed a charming little silver hummingbird hanging from a chain around the woman's neck. "That's a very pretty necklace."

Jenny reached up to clasp the silver bird, seemed like she wanted to say something, but then sported what seemed like a forced smile, instead. "Thank you."

Blythe offered a similar smile. There didn't seem to be more to say on the subject. "Would you like to sign the guest register?" She pushed the ledger forward.

"Sure." Jenny picked up the pen and signed her name and the time. "I know my mother booked a room with two double beds, but I was wondering if I could have something a little more—"

"Intimate?"

"I guess. It's just that, seeing two beds would—"

"I completely understand. And I'll be glad to credit you for the difference at the end of your stay." Blythe turned and plucked a key from the old-fashioned rack of pigeonholes behind the desk. "I think you'll be quite happy in Seaside. The view is very nice."

"I'm sure I'll love it."

Jenny turned, taking in the lobby. "You have such a pretty place."

"Thank you."

Jenny stepped over to the end table at the left end of the couch. "Hello, kitty-cat. What's your name?" She scratched the top of the cat's head, and she began to purr loudly.

"That's Martha. She usually greets guests when they arrive, but she seems to be off duty right now."

Jenny laughed, but it had a hollow ring to it.

"By the way, we're having a 'girls only' weekend, which is probably why your mother chose to come during our off-season."

Jenny turned to face her. "Oh?"

"Yes. And to celebrate, we're having afternoon tea for all the guests. Most of them are at dinner right now, but they'll be returning soon. I'll be setting out a decanter of sherry and glasses shortly. If you're up to it, you might want to wander in during the evening to meet the others."

"Maybe," Jenny said noncommittedly.

"The tea is set for two o'clock in the dining room. I hope you'll be able to make it."

"I don't know. I mean, I don't have any real plans so ... maybe."

"Well, think about it," Blythe suggested.

"I will."

Blythe offered her most sincere smile. "Your room is just down that hall—" She went to leave the reception desk, but Jenny waved her to stay put.

"I can find it if you'll just point the way."

Blythe indicated the hall leading off the lobby. "The last room on the left. Please let me know if you need anything."

"I will, thank you. "

Blythe watched her guest retreat down the hall and shook her head. She well remembered the heartache from losing a loved one. Eventually one got used to the loss, but never really got over it. But then she smiled. Though Jenny's heart had been broken, perhaps the manor could work its magic on her.

Blythe crossed her fingers and hoped so.

Jenny walked down the carpeted hallway and paused before the door with a small painting of a beach at sunrise—or was it sunset?—attached to it. She slipped the key into the lock and opened the door. Despite the fact she'd changed rooms at the last moment, the lamps on either side of the bed were ablaze, as though to welcome her. She'd seen photos of several of the inn's rooms and suites on the website and had been duly impressed, but this room wasn't among them. Its charm instantly won her over and she was immediately seized with a profound sense of peace.

Jenny stepped inside, trailing her suitcase behind her, closed the door, and paused to drink in her surroundings. The walls had been painted pale blue. The furniture was all white, with a four-poster double bed covered in a sumptuous white bedspread with a lacy dust ruffle looking like a slip poking out from beneath a wedding gown. Four linen-clad white pillows, also adorned in lace, sat at the top of the bed, while a faded counterpane of fat pink roses on a background of pale blue lay across the bottom of the bed. Pretty prints—or were they oil paintings?—of roses adorned the walls. Though it was a precious room, she found it entirely to her liking. For a brief moment, she almost felt happy.

And then she remembered the frantic phone call she'd received two months before. How she'd punched 911 into her cell phone. Arriving at her mother's home, she found that although the paramedics had arrived in record time, her mother —her closest confidant—was already gone.

She'd never even had an opportunity to say good-bye.

Jenny brushed away a tear, cleared her throat, and decided to further investigate the room that would be her home away from home for the next two nights. At the foot of the bed was a trunk that, upon opening, proved to store additional pillows and blankets. The top was padded in a floral pattern that complimented the rest of the tranquil room.

She wandered into the bathroom that not only sported a claw-foot soaker tub, but an old marble-topped vanity that had once been a dresser. A white porcelain cherub hoisted a large scallop shell acting as a soap dish on its shoulder. Jenny picked up the small bar from it and took a sniff. Ah … apricot! Her first inclination was to kick off her shoes and unwind. A jar of bath salts sat on a small shelf above the tub. Maybe she'd indulge herself and take a long relaxing soak before going to bed.

One thing she hadn't noticed upon entering the room was a television. She left the bathroom to make sure and, as she thought, there was no TV. However, there was a clock radio with glowing red numerals sitting on the right nightstand. Later on, maybe she'd see if she could tune in an oldies station. That was what her mother would have done.

Charming though the room was, there were no books or magazines—nothing much to do—and she hadn't thought to bring anything of that nature to entertain herself. She'd seen pictures of the library online, which housed floor-to-ceiling bookshelves. Perhaps she'd find something there to bring back to the room and read.

After hanging her coat in the closet and unpacking her night shirt and toiletries, Jenny locked her room, but instead of crossing the hall for the library, the sound of voices from the vicinity of the lobby caused her to pause. She crept forward, but saw no sign of the inn's hostess at the reception desk. However, two elderly ladies—their backs to her—sat before the lobby's massive fireplace where a number of big logs blazed brightly. She hesitated to interrupt their conversation and stood still until their conversation lagged, then tip-toed forward. Reluctant to startle them, Jenny cleared her throat. The two gray-haired ladies turned.

"Hello," one of them said brightly.

"Hi."

"Come and join us," said the other, and with a sherry glass in hand, indicated the empty chair to their right. Jenny took it.

These ladies were pretty darned old—at least to Jenny's untrained eye. Both her grandmothers had died before she was born, so she'd never known the unconditional love that such family members were supposed to have given.

"I'm Jenny Taylor."

"It's so nice to meet you," said the first old lady. "I'm Lavinia Albright, and this," she indicated the other woman "is my dear friend, Maude Dodge."

"Hi," Jenny said shyly.

"Jenny is such a pretty name. Not like the awful monikers my father saddled me with," said Maude. "I was named after Daddy's elderly aunt."

"Och! Horrible names," Lavinia agreed. "I was named after my grandmother. I used to wish my name was Debbie. Isn't that a fun-sounding name?"

"And I always wanted to be Betty," her friend said wistfully. She looked at Jenny. "Did you ever wish to be named something else?"

Jenny shrugged. "When I was little, I sometimes pretended my name was Tiffany. She was the smartest, most popular girl in my class."

"Bright, no doubt—just like this lamp," Maude said and giggled.

Jenny noticed that the inn's mascot had abandoned her former perch and was nowhere to be found."

"Would you like a glass of sherry?" Lavinia asked.

"I've never had one before."

"Then you're in for a treat." Lavinia poured the mahogany-colored liquid into one of the stemmed crystal glasses and handed it to Jenny, who took a hearty sip—and began to choke.

"Tiny sips—tiny sips!" Maude advised while Jenny continued to cough and wheeze.

"It's a little harsh," Jenny managed.

"Nonsense. This is *cream* sherry. Goes down much easier than the other stuff. By the time you finish your glass, you'll come to love it, too."

Jenny doubted that.

"Remember the time you got sick on cream sherry?" Maude said, giving her friend a dig.

"Do I ever." Lavinia sank farther into the comfortable-looking leather couch. "It wasn't too long after Jerry and I got married. One of mother's friends gave her a bottle of sherry she'd received as a Christmas present. Mother didn't drink, but she didn't want to offend her friend, so she gave me the bottle. Well, I wasn't much of a drinker back then, either—"

"You lush you," Maude interrupted.

"I thought sherry was just wine—not fortified."

"Fortified?" Jenny asked.

"Much stronger," Lavinia clarified. "So Jerry and I figured we'd kill the bottle."

"I wish I'd been there," Maude said, once again captured by giggles.

"We'd guzzled just about the whole bottle and were pretty

loopy, but Jerry insisted on getting supper ready. He always was a better cook than me, anyway."

"What did you have?" Jenny asked.

"Polish sausage. I don't remember what else was on my plate. It all went down." She raised her hand high into the air, and then quickly let it sail toward the floor. "And then it all came right back up—along with half the bottle of sherry."

Maude slapped her right thigh, laughing outright now.

Jenny wasn't sure what to say.

"To this day, I can't even stand the *thought* of Polish sausage, and it was one of my favorite treats before that night," Lavinia lamented. Maude wiped tears from her eyes, still unable to stop laughing.

Lavinia sipped her sherry, occasionally rolling her eyes in her friend's direction until Maude was finally able to calm down. "She does this all the time," Lavinia muttered confidentially.

Jenny still couldn't come up with anything appropriate to say.

Lavinia took up the conversational ball once more. "So, you came here for the girls-weekend?"

"I didn't even know about it. My mother and I were supposed to come here to—" She paused, "for a weekend getaway. I didn't know it was a girls-only affair until I checked in."

"Where's your mother? In her room?" Maude asked.

Jenny shook her head. "She passed away."

"Oh, I'm so sorry."

"Me, too," Maude echoed, and reached over to pat Jenny's hand.

"It was sudden," Jenny said, and again reached for the little hummingbird charm that hung from around her neck. She didn't want to discuss her situation and decided to change the course of the conversation. "Do you two have children?"

"I've got three," Lavinia said.

"I've got two—a boy and a girl, although they haven't been

children in decades. I guess a mother always thinks of her children as—well, children," Maude said.

"Do they live near you?"

"Not anymore," Lavinia said, "which is probably just as well. After they flew the coop, they never came to see me and Jerry much anyway. When Jerry died, my oldest couldn't even be bothered to come to the funeral—he had a big presentation at work—but he called and sent me a card. I guess he figured that was enough. I cut him out of the will. In fact, I've decided not to leave a nickel to anyone. I'm going to spend it all on travel and good times. I only wish Jerry was here to enjoy the fruits of his labor."

"You go, girl!" Maude encouraged her BFF.

Jenny blinked. "How about you?"

"I lost my husband about five years ago. My kids are okay. They call at least once a week. They live not five minutes from me, but they're very busy with their own families."

"That's terrible," Jenny said. She'd been very close to her mother, who'd pushed her out of the nest because she was worried Jenny would one day end up taking care of her—like she'd had to do for her own mother—and didn't want that to happen.

Maude shook her head and sighed. "My daughter was very strict with my granddaughter—much stricter than I ever was. She was a soccer mom and loved it! I mean, it was unnatural. Poor Emily didn't even like soccer, but Leslie—that's my daughter—never missed a game. She took vacation time off just to see practices. That's just not normal."

"I'll say," Lavinia agreed, taking another sip.

"So was it any wonder that Emily's first time up to bat with a boy, she was knocked up?"

"Don't you mean knocked out?"

"No—she was knocked *up*. I'm now a great grandmother. Can you imagine that? I'm much too young to be a great grandmother."

"Well, not really, dear," Lavinia chided.

Maude leveled a scorching glance at her friend before continuing. "The way little Caleb gets dragged between my daughter's house and being dumped on his father every weekend, is it any wonder he's a handful? But he's Leslie's problem, not mine—thank goodness."

Jenny managed another tiny sip of her sherry. Boy, these ladies didn't mind dishing their family secrets. Again, she decided to steer the conversation in another direction. "Are you going anywhere after this weekend?"

"On Monday, we're heading to Boston to catch a flight to Dublin where we'll meet up with a bus tour and travel around the country for two weeks."

"We're going to kiss the Blarney Stone," Maude declared.

"You have to do it hanging upside down," Lavinia put in. "Doesn't that sound like fun?"

Not really. Jenny wondered about the bacteria that clung to the stone. What if someone who had a cold or a virus kissed it? They could infect untold hundreds of unsuspecting tourists. If she ever went to the Emerald Isle, she vowed to eat some Blarney cheese, not kiss the stone.

"How many other guests are here for the weekend?" Jenny asked.

"Four other ladies. I believe they're sorority sisters. They arrived here just after we did. They went out to dinner," Lavinia said.

"We ordered in a seafood pizza. It was wonderful. Have you eaten?" Maude asked.

"Yes. I stopped at a clam shack before coming here. I'd originally thought I might go for lobster, but the shack seemed a better option for a woman alone."

"I take it you have no siblings?" Lavinia asked.

"It was just me and my mom. She and my dad divorced when I was just a baby. He was never a presence in my life."

"That's so sad," Maude said.

"I've got a couple of half-siblings, but they live on the west coast. I've never even met them."

"Do you want to?"

Jenny shrugged. "Not really."

"Do you have aunts and uncles?" Maude asked.

Jenny shook her head. "My mom was an only child, too."

"Do you have *anyone*?" Lavinia asked.

"Just my best friend, Missy. She had a wedding to go to this weekend and couldn't change her plans."

"She's not much of a best friend then," Maude muttered into her glass of sherry.

Jenny kind of—sort of—felt the same way. Why had Missy felt more loyalty to someone she hadn't seen in years instead of the friend who was a part of her life just about every day?

It did no good to think about such things.

Lavinia drained her glass and glanced at the watch on her wrist. "Look at the time, Maude."

"You're right. It's much later than I thought."

"Are you ladies going to bed so early?"

"Oh, no," Lavinia said. "But we hope to get in a couple of episodes of Gilmore Giles before bedtime."

"Do you have a TV in your room?" Jenny asked.

"No, but I brought my laptop and packed the last three seasons worth of DVDs. No matter how bad the TV is on our travels, we always bring some kind of entertainment with us."

"And I packed all five seasons of Boston Legal as a backup. That Denny Crane is a hoot," Maude chimed in.

Oh-kay.

The ladies stood in unison.

"It's been lovely to meet you, Jenny. We may not be about in the morning as we've booked a personal tour of the island, but we'll be at the tea. You will be there, won't you?" Lavinia asked.

"I haven't decided," Jenny answered truthfully.

Both ladies pursed their lips at the declaration.

"As you wish, dear," Maude said, "but I hope you'll opt to come. There is strength in numbers."

What was that supposed to mean?

"It's been very nice to meet you," Jenny said, placed her now-empty glass on the old blanket chest that served as a coffee table, and stood. "I hope we get to talk again." She left the statement open-ended, unsure if she wanted company for the rest of the weekend. Then again, she'd been alone far too much during the past two months, which had been painful to endure.

"We will," Maude said with conviction. "Good night," the women wished her.

"Good night," Jenny said, gave the ladies a smile and a nod, and watched them leave the lobby. Once they'd disappeared down the hall, she ambled over to the bookshelves. Among the volumes were some children's classics. Jenny's mother had often spoken of her favorite book from childhood: Frances Hodgson Burnett's *The Secret Garden*. It was the reason she'd taken up gardening as a hobby. Their small yard had always been rife with blooms all summer long, and their vegetable patch had fed them fresh food in the summer, and frozen and canned treats the rest of the year. It all seemed like a lot of work to a child and teenager, but now the thought of not having her mother and a garden to work in this summer made the upcoming months seem just a little bleaker.

Jenny hefted the book in her hand. For some reason, she'd always balked at the idea of reading a story set in the early twentieth century. Now she wished she had, because she knew it would have pleased her mother.

Once again, she clasped the hummingbird charm at her neck. "I'll read it now, Mom. Or at least I'll try."

Tucking the tome under her arm, Jenny started back for her pretty room, hoping she'd soon be entranced by the story of a lonely little orphan girl and how a secret garden saved her.

CHAPTER 4

The sky was still dark when Blythe entered her kitchen the next morning. She paused for a moment to listen to the rain pounding on the roof. Somehow, she always found that to be a comforting sound. Comforting for her, but inconvenient for her guests who'd hoped for fair weather on their trip to the island.

Martha rubbed her body against Blythe's ankles and cried piteously.

"Yes, I know you're hungry. I'll be right with you." But the first order of business was to fire up the ivory-colored AGA cooker that was the focal point of her large country kitchen.

Blythe puttered around, feeding Martha, then taking a dozen assorted muffins and an apple strudel from the freezer. They'd thaw in time for the sorority sisters to have their breakfast, but she also intended to make Eggs Benedict, as well.

The coffee was brewing and Blythe began to assemble the ingredients for the cake she intended to bake that would be the featured dessert for the afternoon tea later that day, when footsteps approached.

Blythe turned. "Good morning, Jenny. You're up early."

"I'm afraid I didn't sleep well," she said, looking weary. She was dressed for the day, holding onto a book.

"I'm so sorry. I've never had any complaints about—"

"No, no!' Jenny hurriedly interrupted. "It wasn't the bed—it's very comfortable. And my room is absolutely perfect. I had a hard time falling asleep, is all. I read until quite late, and then I woke up an hour ago and just couldn't fall back to sleep. I guess I've got a lot on my mind."

Blythe offered her a sympathetic smile. "The coffee will be ready in a few minutes, unless you'd rather have tea or cocoa."

"Coffee is fine. It's what I usually have for breakfast. My mother drank tea."

"What kind?"

"Either English or Irish breakfast tea. She liked it strong."

Blythe grinned. "As do I." She took two hand-thrown pottery mugs down from the cupboard and set them on the counter near the Bun-O-Matic coffeemaker. "How do you take yours?"

"With just milk."

"So do I." Stepping around Martha, who had parked herself by the warm cooker, Blythe took a small pitcher from the cupboard, filled it with milk from the fridge, and set it on the counter. "Are you ready for breakfast?"

Jenny smiled. "If I eat now, I'll just want another breakfast in an hour or so."

"I hear you."

Jenny pointed to the sack of flour, can of crushed pineapple, bananas, and cinnamon all lined up before her. "What's all that for?"

"The cake I'm going to make for tea this afternoon. It'll be the crowning glory."

"I like cake—maybe a little too much," Jenny admitted.

"If you ask me, it's one of life's greatest pleasures. Nobody ever got fat eating just one piece, but too many people deny themselves the enjoyment."

"I admit, I don't bake for myself because I'm afraid I'd pig out."

"Cake freezes quite well, as do most baked items."

"Like those muffins?" Jenny asked, eyeing the bounty set out to thaw.

"Exactly. Would you like one? They're apple crumble or carrot cake."

"The apple sounds heavenly."

Blythe took a small plate from the cupboard, placed a muffin on it, popped it into the microwave, giving it thirty seconds, and then offered it to Jenny. She poured coffee for both of them.

Jenny peeled the paper wrapping from the muffin and broke off a portion of the top, taking a bite. As she chewed, her smile widened. "Oh, that is fantastic."

"The recipe is on the manor's website. Just click on the link marked EXTRAS."

"I will definitely do that when I get home. Maybe I'll make a batch and take them to work. I'm sure my officemates and the guys in the warehouse would love them."

"Do you like your job?" Blythe asked, hauling the big mixer away from the wall so that she had better access to it."

"Yeah, I do. I work in a lumber yard—of all places. I'm an expeditor. I keep track of what inventory we have on hand, arrange to purchase what we need on a day-to-day basis, and keep track of special orders. It's rather meticulous work that drove the last person who had the job crazy, but I thrive on that kind of detail."

"Being happy in one's work is one of the greatest joys in life."

"Are you happy?" Jenny asked.

Blythe felt a wellspring of bliss envelope her. "Taking care of the manor and serving my guests is incredibly rewarding. When visitors arrive stressed and unhappy, I hope my small efforts bring them comfort and respite. Can there be any greater purpose?"

Jenny shrugged. "I guess not." She nibbled on more of her

muffin. "I should leave you to your work."

"Will you come to the tea this afternoon?"

"I guess it depends on the weather." The rain still hammered the roof. "I made a list of places I thought I might like to see, but now that I'm here—and the weather is so crappy—I might just stay here at the manor for the day. It's such a peaceful place. It just feels good to be here."

"I'm glad you feel that way. I've heard some say they think the house and grounds have healing properties. Others claim there's an almost mystical calming aspect here they feel in no other place on Earth."

"Do you believe that?" Jenny asked, sounding skeptical.

Blythe turned to retrieve her measuring cups and spoons. "Sometimes."

Jenny picked up her cup. "I'm keeping you from your work. I think I'll go sit in the lobby."

"Would you like me to put a few extra logs on the fire?"

"Oh, no. I'm just going to try to finish this book and drink my coffee."

"Please let me know if you need anything."

"I will, thank you."

Blythe watched her young lodger make her way through the dining room and into the lobby, and then turned back to her workspace. She enjoyed measuring the ingredients for the recipes she made and anticipated the pleasure the final product would elicit from her guests. This cake, in particular, could be inspirational, and even if it wasn't, the ladies would enjoy it and the conviviality in which it was shared.

Martha got up, stretched, turned around twice, and then settled back down in front of the stove. Blythe couldn't help but smile—at her cat, and because she had an inkling of just how meaningful that afternoon's tea was likely to be. With just a little magic, the spirit of kindness and empathy that would touch the heart of one of her guests—the one who needed it most.

CHAPTER 5

Jenny finished her muffin and then curled up on the big leather couch intending to read, but the fire's glow and the cozy atmosphere did what her pretty room hadn't been able to do. Her muscles relaxed and her eyes grew heavy. She rested her head on the arm of the sofa, intending to close her eyes for just a moment, but immediately fell into an exhausted sleep.

When she awoke, the sky was a dismal gray and two hours had passed. Someone had spread a hand-crocheted afghan over her. The aroma of baking seemed to fill the house and the fire in the hearth still burned merrily, as though new logs had been added just moments before.

Sitting upright, Jenny removed the throw, folded it, and placed it on the back of the couch, then grabbed her book and spread it open on her lap at the place where'd she left off hours earlier. But before she could begin to read, she heard the sound of soft footsteps.

They came to the dining room one by one—in their pajamas. Silly pajamas. Pajamas imprinted with cats, with dogs, with parrots, and even pink elephants. They were older than her by at least twenty years. They were loud, boisterous, and obviously having fun—a lot of fun. They had to be the sorority sisters that Lavinia and Maude had spoken of the evening before. They sounded more like biological siblings.

Jenny tried not to pay attention to the laughter, tried not to think about how much fun she and Missy could have had *if* her friend had decided to join her. She tried to concentrate on the words on the page before her, but found it nearly impossible. Her stomach gave a loud growl and she glanced at the clock on the mantle. It had been a little more than two hours since she'd eaten that wonderful muffin. Perhaps she'd go sit at a table overlooking the lawn and the garden beyond and have a real breakfast. Yes— that's what she'd do.

She got up and walked from the lobby to the dining room and took a seat at a table set for two, the empty chair opposite her once again emphasizing her loss. Should she wait there for her hostess to wait on her or go to the kitchen to request something to eat? A carafe of coffee stood on the big round table to Jenny's right where the women sat, and all of them seemed to be nursing cups. The rest of the muffins and strudel she'd seen earlier in the kitchen were piled on pretty cake plates. Jenny eyed the carafe. Should she ask if she could pour herself a cup?

"Did you hear about Crystal?" asked one of the women. Jenny looked away, afraid they might think her nosy if she continued to stare. But it was only seconds later when her gaze strayed back in that direction that she noticed the woman had fuchsia colored nails that contrasted nicely with her paler pink elephant PJs.

"No," the other three chorused.

"Divorce number two is on the way?" she practically sang.

"Really? But I thought she and this latest bozo were supposed to be a match made in heaven."

"More like H-E double hockey sticks," the first one said and laughed. The others joined in with her.

"Honestly, what was she thinking marrying a three-time loser with six illegitimate kids?"

"That love would keep them together?" the woman with the kitty jammies chimed in, and then lifted her spoon as though it was a microphone and started singing that oldies tune Jenny had heard from her mother's kitchen radio about a million times while growing up. They all broke into helpless giggles.

Jenny opened her book, lowered her head and tried to read, but couldn't seem to concentrate on the words. She looked out over the soggy lawn as the rain continued to pelt the windows. Outside the window hung a hummingbird feeder swaying in the strong breeze. One of the tiny birds struggled to dip his beak into the little plastic flower to drink the nectar. *What a tenacious creature*, she thought, and again reached for the charm that hung from the chain around her neck.

The women at the other table continued to converse.

"Is it too early to plan our fall get together?" asked the one in the kitty PJs.

"It's gotta be after school starts so I have time to freeze enough meals to keep the kids and Mike in food while I'm gone. Otherwise, he'll feed them pizza and candy and when I get home they'll be bouncing off the ceiling."

"It takes you four months to put together two day's worth of meals?" asked parrot woman.

"Yes. You know I have a *huge* procrastination problem."

"There are drugs for that, you know," said the one in the pink elephant jammies.

"Really?"

"Don't be ridiculous. Of course there aren't!" But that didn't stop them all from laughing once again.

When the laughter died, a conspicuous silence fell over the room, Jenny heard one of the women whisper. "Do you think we should ask that young lady to join us?"

Jenny cringed inwardly and looked away. The truth was, she

felt terribly lonely. That coming to Blythe Cove Manor alone may have been a big mistake. And what if they decided not to invite her to join them? Should she run back to her room and hide for the rest of the day?

"Excuse me," asked the woman in the parrot pajamas, who was suddenly standing beside her. "But would you like to join us for breakfast?"

Startled, Jenny hesitated.

"I promise, we don't bite." And to prove it, the woman removed a partial plate from her mouth that concealed her lack of four upper front teeth.

Jenny couldn't help herself; she laughed.

Apparently, that was exactly the reaction the woman had anticipated, for she popped her faux teeth back into her mouth and joined in gleefully. "I lost them when I was twelve," she explained. "My dad warned me not to ride my bike on that rainy day, but I knew better. I stopped fast, flew over the handlebars, and landed on my mouth. Good-bye so-called permanent teeth. That aside, our invitation is sincere."

Jenny smiled. "Thank you. I'd love to." She picked up her book and was welcomed to the big round table with a cacophony of what sounded like sincere hellos.

"I'm Pam," said parrot woman. "And this is Lisa, Amy, and Tracy."

"I'm Jenny."

"Hi, Jenny," the women said in unison.

"It'll be a lot easier for us to get to know you than for you to get to know this gang in one fell swoop," Pam said. "So tell us a little about yourself."

"There's not much to tell. I was supposed to be here with my mother, but she passed away suddenly about two months ago."

"Aw," the women lamented as one.

Jenny gave them the Cliff Notes version of her life, more interested to hear about each of them.

Pam took on the role of Mistress of Ceremonies. "Lisa is a microbiologist. She's doing research at Columbia University and also knits goofy dishcloths."

"They're very useful," Lisa protested, while her three friends rolled their eyes and made gagging noises.

"Amy's a veterinarian and teaches at Cornell University."

"I specialize in equines—should you ever need my services."

Jenny wasn't quite sure what that meant. "I live in a tiny apartment. No room for even a guinea pig, although I've been considering moving back into my mom's house."

"Tracy is a Special Ed teacher in Boston. She stumbled across Blythe Cove Manor last summer and said we *had* to come here for one of our retreats." Tracy bowed her head, as though welcoming the credit. "And I'm the PR director of a Fortune 500 company—which shall be nameless in case you might try to sue me."

Jenny doubted that. "How often do you meet?"

"Not nearly enough!" Pam said, and the table broke into whoops of agreement. "Ideally, we'd like to get together four times a year, but that's not always possible."

"Lavinia—another guest—thought you ladies might be sorority sisters."

"She's right. We all met in college about a million years ago. We've been friends ever since."

"You all have really impressive jobs." Jenny forced a laugh. "Makes what I do seem so inconsequential?"

"Why?" Lisa asked, sounding puzzled.

"Working in a lumber yard doesn't change the world."

"Tell that to people who want to build homes," Tracy pointed out.

"Do you like the work?" Pam asked.

"I do."

"Can you support yourself?" Amy asked.

"I make good money."

"Then what's the problem?" Lisa asked.

Jenny gave an embarrassed laugh. "I guess there isn't one."

"Breakfast is served," Blythe called, swooping into the dining room and carrying a large tray. She set it down at one of the nearby empty tables and doled out the plates with the promised Eggs Benedict. She even had one prepared for Jenny, who picked up her fork with trepidation. She'd never eaten the dish before.

"Can I get you ladies anything else?"

"More coffee?" Pam said hopefully.

"Of course." Blythe picked up the carafe and the tray and headed back to the kitchen.

"I've never had Eggs Benedict before," Jenny said.

"Then you're in for a treat," Amy said.

Jenny cut into the sauce covered egg, its bright yellow steaming yolk gushing out and soaking into the toasted English muffin beneath it. She had never eaten so runny a yolk, but as the other women were tucking in and moaning in ecstasy, she swallowed and took her first bite … and loved it. She chewed and swallowed. "Oh, wow—I never knew an egg could taste so good."

"It's the hollandaise sauce," Tracy said and wiped a napkin around her mouth. "And this is the best I've ever tasted."

"I made it myself," Blythe said as she returned with the refilled pot and a new cup for Jenny.

"What makes it so special?" Tracy asked.

"Nothing. It's just a standard recipe."

"Well then, you make it better than anyone else on the planet." Amy took another bite, closed her eyes, and moaned in ecstasy.

Blythe refilled their cups and retreated once again.

"What are your plans for today?" Lisa asked, looking straight at Jenny.

"I thought about driving around the island, but since the weather is so nasty, I think I'm going to stay in and read instead. It's not something I get a lot of time to do at home."

"We're going shopping in Edgartown, if you'd like to join us," Pam asked.

"Oh, that's very sweet of you, but it sounds like you ladies only get a couple of days together a year. I don't want to intrude."

"You wouldn't be intruding," Lisa said, eyeing the plate filled with muffins.

Jenny hesitated. "Thank you, but I think I'll stick with my plans. Besides, I'll see you all at the tea this afternoon."

"That's right," Lisa said. "I think I'd better stick to the eggs. I wonder what Blythe will serve. I bet it'll be decadent."

"She mentioned making a special cake. It sure smelled good," Jenny offered.

"That's a very pretty charm on your necklace," Amy said. "Where did you get it?"

Jenny wasn't up to explaining about her mother yet again. "It was special ordered."

"I'll bet my daughter would like one of those on her charm bracelet."

I hope you live forever so she'll never need to have one, Jenny thought.

"Before the end of the weekend, we've got to talk about my kitchen reno," Tracy said, launching into a new topic of conversation. She ended up retrieving her iPad so that she could show everyone the Pinterest board she'd put together, eliciting everyone's opinions and votes on tile, flooring, and even the brand of dishwasher she considered buying.

It was fun to see the dynamics among this band of long-time friends, and Jenny wished she had been blessed with such long-standing friendships. Well, she was a lot younger than them. Maybe she'd one day be able to claim the same experience.

All too soon breakfast was over and the women went back to their respective rooms to get ready for the big shopping expedition. Twenty minutes later, they called a cheery good-bye before trundling out in the rain with umbrellas borrowed from the manor.

The big lobby felt enormous and deadly quiet after the echoes of their laughter dissipated.

Jenny took her seat in front of the fire, which still seemed to be burning without ever having been restocked with wood, and sat down once again to read.

The clock ticked loudly.

It would be a long day until the other guests returned for afternoon tea.

She opened the book, returning to the story of a little girl, a garden, and how friendship saved not only her, but those she came to love the most.

Blythe fussed with the vase full of pink and white tulips that the local florist had delivered not ten minutes before, making sure they looked their loveliest for her guests. Everything looked perfect. She'd used her prettiest tablecloth, vintage china—a different setting at every place—the silver had been polished until it glowed, and now all she had to do was wait for her guests to file in.

Leaving the dining room, she hurried back to the kitchen to put the big kettle on the Aga. There would be three pots of tea on the table for the ladies to choose from; Earl Grey, black tea, and white tea. The sandwiches were egg-with-cress, and cucumber. Keeping to her garden theme, she'd made cookies with lavender, rose water, and cut-out cookies in the shape of daisies, sunflowers, and cherry blossoms.

Donning a fresh apron, Blythe decided that all was ready—and just in time, for she heard her first guests filing in the manor's dining room: Lavinia and Maude.

"Did you have a nice day touring the island," Blythe asked.

"Unfortunately, no. The unseasonable weather put a crimp in our plans," Lavinia lamented.

"I'm so sorry."

"That was partially our fault. We now understand why there is a season to come visit the island. We like what we saw enough to decide to come back during the summer—that is, if you aren't already fully booked."

"I'll look through the reservations and let you know by tomorrow morning what's still available."

"We'd appreciate it," Maude said, and turned her attention to the pretty table. "Everything looks so beautiful. Did you calligraphy these place cards yourself?"

"Yes. I hope you don't mind, but I mixed up the names so that just about everyone would get to make a new friend."

"What a wonderful idea," Lavinia agreed. "Will sweet Jenny be joining us this afternoon?"

"Yes, I believe she mentioned to one of the other guests that she would."

"Oh, good," Maude said, "Because when Lavinia and I stopped at a gift shop, we decided to buy her a little something. Nothing big, just a token of friendship."

"That's very sweet of you."

Lavinia set her large purse down on the chair before her name card and opened it, withdrawing a rectangular-shaped package wrapped in pretty, old-fashioned rose-patterned paper.

"Shall I set it on the sideboard?" Blythe asked.

"Yes, thank you," She handed the parcel to Blythe who set it aside, but far enough from the stands where small candles would keep the teapots warm. "If you'd like to sit down, I'll bring in the tea."

By the time Blythe had set all three pots of tea on a tray, she heard more voices coming from the dining room. Two of the sorority sisters had arrived. They, too, held wrapped gifts.

"These are for Jenny," Pam said, placing another two small packages on the sideboard.

"That was very thoughtful of you," Blythe said. "The other

ladies," she indicated Lavinia and Maude, "also brought Jenny a gift."

"I lost my mother a little over a year ago. For Jenny to have made this trip on her own—the one she and her mom were supposed to take together, and so soon after her mother's death … well, I don't think I would have been able to do it."

"Me, either," Tracy said.

Their other friends entered the dining room, and they, too, were carrying small wrapped packages. "Looks like great minds think alike," Amy said as she and Lisa added their gifts to the pile.

Blythe introduced everyone and then excused herself to put some soft, background music on the stereo. When she returned, she saw that Jenny had just arrived. She hurried to intercept her. "It looks like you're the guest of honor."

"I don't understand."

"It *is* your birthday," Blythe whispered.

Jenny's jaw dropped. "Yes, but—how did you know?"

"Caroline told me."

Jenny did a classic double take.

"When she booked the reservation," Blythe hurriedly explained. "Would it be all right if I told the others?"

"Oh. I—I don't know. It might make everyone feel awkward."

"Or it might give them something else to celebrate. Everybody loves a birthday party."

Jenny looked unsure, and perhaps a little embarrassed. "Okay."

Blythe beckoned Jenny forward. "Come and sit down."

"Hey, there she is," Pam called. "We've been waiting for you."

"Sit here," Blythe said, steering Jenny toward the only empty place at the table. "Would everyone like some tea?"

Blythe told them about the various teas, listened to their preferences, and began to pour.

Like her mother, Jenny asked for black tea. She picked up the cup. "Oh, what a pretty hummingbird. It's gorgeous." She looked down, delighted. "And the plate matches, too."

"I thought you might like it."

Jenny reached to grasp the hummingbird charm around her neck. "Thank you."

Blythe poured the tea. "Would you ladies like to take a few minutes to enjoy your tea, or shall I bring out the sandwiches and scones?"

"It's been an eternity since breakfast," Lisa said. "I vote for food. Any other takers?"

The reply was unanimous, and Blythe retreated to the kitchen to retrieve the three-tiered plates she'd already assembled, plus the butter, clotted cream, and small pots of jam. When she returned, the reaction was universal.

"That looks heavenly. Where's my camera?" Pam said.

"I'm going to put this on my Facebook page," Lisa said, already aiming her cell phone at the plates nearest her.

"Instagram for me," said Amy.

"We should encourage the ladies at church to put on a lovely tea, Maude," said Lavinia, and she, too, was aiming her cell phone at one of the plates.

The room was suddenly filled with laughter and cameras clicking as everyone took pictures and selfies with their food before they sat down for the serious business of eating.

Blythe stayed in the background, but kept busy refilling teacups, bringing in more sandwiches, and another tiered plate filled with cookies, while the women got to know one another. They laughed, shared personal histories, and everyone seemed to have a funny story to share. All but Jenny, who appeared to be caught up in the camaraderie, smiling—as though her troubles had been forgotten—almost forgotten. She was about to get the cake when Pam, who seemed to be the spokeswoman for her sorority sisters, rose to her feet.

"I don't know about you guys, but I've had a wonderful time

getting to know you, Jenny, Lavinia, and Maude. Somehow, it feels like in a very short space of time, we've all gotten to be friends."

"Hear, hear," Lisa chimed in.

"And while the weather might still be frightful," and as she said that, they heard the rumble of thunder from overhead, which elicited another round of laughter, "the food, and the company, has certainly been delightful."

Everyone raised their teacups in salute. She took two steps back and plucked one of the wrapped gifts from the sideboard. "And that's why I'd like to present this to Jenny."

Jenny looked up, surprised. "What?"

"It's just a small token of friendship."

"A present—for me?"

"Sure. And now that I've met Lavinia and Maude, I wish I'd gotten two more," she said, smiling.

Jenny stared at the thin, square package. "I don't know what to say."

"Don't say anything—just rip off the paper!" Tracy encouraged.

Blythe leaned in to watch as Jenny slid her thumb under a piece of tape and pulled off the wrapping. Jenny took one look at the gift and smiled. "Oh, my—it's an address book, with a hummingbird on the cover!"

"I've already put my address in it. Why don't you circulate it around the table and get everyone else's?"

Jenny's smile could have lit up the room. "Thank you."

"I can come up with some paper for the rest of you," Blythe said, and was immediately taken up on the offer. She moved to the sideboard and found a pad and a number of pens and distributed them around the table.

"Here's another one," Lisa said, and plucked another present from the pile, handing it to Jenny.

"Again, I don't know what to say."

"You might not like it, so don't say anything until you see it," Lisa advised.

Once again, Jenny was careful removing the paper from another thin rectangular item. "Oh, my goodness. Thank you." She smiled and then held it up—a small book entitled *A Hummingbird's Garden*. "My mother was an avid gardener, I always thought I had a brown thumb, but this will encourage me to try my hand at establishing a patch my mother would be proud of."

Warm applause followed that statement.

It was Lavinia's turn to rise and select the biggest box from the pile. "This is from Maude and me. Perhaps it will be a welcome addition to your new garden." She handed the gift to Jenny, who proceeded to unwrap it. Once the paper was removed, her smile widened.

"A hummingbird feeder," she said, and showed it off.

"We hope you'll get as many hours of enjoyment from this as the two of us have had with our own," Maude said.

Jenny opened the last two presents: a hummingbird clock from Amy, and tiny blue hummingbird earrings from Tracy.

"I'm overwhelmed by the kindness all you ladies have shown me," Jenny began. It was then that Blythe slipped back into the kitchen to grab the cake, but not until she'd lit the ten or so candles that decorated its circumference. She walked slowly into the dining room, carefully balancing the cake stand. She set it down beside Jenny.

"What you ladies didn't know, is that today is Jenny's twenty-fourth birthday."

"Happy birthday," the six women called out as one, and then there were whoops of laughter and calls of "you go, girl!" Then Pam began to sing *Happy Birthday to You* and Blythe and the rest of the women joined in.

Jenny's mouth trembled, and her eyes brimmed with tears.

"Thanks—all of you—so much for making what I thought would be a terrible birthday so memorable."

The applause was enthusiastic and Pam called out, "Make a wish and blow out the candles."

Jenny clasped the hummingbird charm on the chain, seemed to take a few moment to contemplate the request, and then blew out the candles.

"Yay!" the women chorused.

"Would you like to make the ceremonial cut?" Blythe asked Jenny, offering her the serrated cake knife.

Jenny took it from her and plunged it into the center of the cake and then relinquished it once again.

"What kind of cake is it?" Lavinia asked.

"I thought that would have been obvious," Blythe said, plopping the first slice on the plate in front of Jenny. "It's hummingbird cake."

For a moment, there was dead silence, and then the dining room again rang with laughter.

"Please don't tell me there are actual hummingbirds in this cake," Tracy said.

Blythe laughed. "No. It's sweet nectar that hummingbirds are attracted to. In this case, the sweetness is crushed pineapple and chopped bananas."

"It tastes heavenly to me," Pam said, and cut another piece of the slice before her.

"Isn't it odd that all of chose to buy Jenny gifts with a hummingbird theme?" Amy said.

"I took my inspiration from the charm on her necklace," Pam said.

"So did I," Lisa said.

"Us, too," Maude affirmed.

"You still haven't told me where you got it," Amy said.

Jenny heaved a sigh. "I ordered it from the funeral parlor that took care of my mother."

Six pairs of eyes blinked.

Jenny reached up, clasping the tiny bird with her left hand. "Some people think it's morbid."

Blythe frowned. "Why?"

"Because it's … it's memorial jewelry," Jenny said, looking down at the cake on the plate before her. "There's a tiny compartment inside that holds cremains." She forced a laugh. "There's a little bit of my mother inside."

"It must bring you a lot of comfort," Blythe said.

"It does, actually. It means my mom is always with me."

Blythe smiled. "I'm sure she is. Were hummingbirds a favorite of Caroline's?"

"Not that I know of. It was the prettiest charm the company offered. For some reason, it just spoke to me."

"Wow," Pam finally said.

"Cool, though," Tracy said.

"What's really cool, is how we all picked up on it. We all bought Jenny something with a hummingbird on it. Blythe made a hummingbird cake," Pam said, "and Jenny's been drinking tea out of a hummingbird cup. Wouldn't it be ironic if that all these hummingbird signs were … well … a sign."

"You mean from Jenny's mother?" Amy asked.

"Maybe *we're* her final gift to Jenny."

"If you believe in that kind of thing," Lisa said skeptically

"I never would have before today, but I think I do now," Jenny said and reached for the charm once again.

"Why don't you tell us all about your mother?" Lavinia suggested.

"Yes," the rest of the women offered.

"As Blythe mentioned, her name was Caroline. She was the nicest, most generous woman on the planet, and I'm proud to be her daughter."

"And I have no doubt," Blythe said, "that she thought the same of you."

Like any hospitality business, checkout time was always hectic. And it was no different on that particular Sunday morning in early May.

After the wonderful tea the afternoon before, all the guests had gathered in the lobby-living room to watch episodes of The Gilmore Girls. It seems that everyone but the birthday girl was well acquainted with the escapades of Lorelei and Rory Gilmore. But the more episodes they watched—with boisterous comments —the more Jenny seemed to identify with at least one of those characters.

The laughter and tears were genuine. And long after the TV and DVD player had been switched off, the women in that room traded stories, ate leftovers, and drank sherry and a couple of bottles of wine that the sorority sisters had supplied.

Blythe was welcomed as "one of the girls," but the truth was, she simply wasn't and was content to stand (or rather sit) on the sidelines, witnessing, but not actually participating in the conviviality. And she was called upon to consult the next year's reservations calendar for the same weekend. She hadn't taken it seriously that these women actually wanted to convene again the next year until every single one of them offered up her credit card to put down a deposit.

Blythe was often sorry to see her guests leave, but the camaraderie and friendships cemented during the preceding thirty-six hours were unprecedented. And it was with sadness that she bid her guests good-bye—until the next year—giving each and every one of them a sincere good-bye hug.

Returning to the reception desk, she found Martha sitting on the guest ledger.

"You look smug."

"*Bbrupt!*" Martha said, and then her gaze traveled to the window that overlooked the garden outside the dining room. There, at the red plastic and glass feeder, was a single hummingbird.

Blythe's Hummingbird Cake Recipe
  3 cups all-purpose flour
  2 cups granulated sugar
  1 teaspoon salt
  1 teaspoon baking soda
  1 teaspoon ground cinnamon
  3 large eggs, beaten
  1½ cups vegetable oil (can substitute unsweetened applesauce)
  1½ teaspoons vanilla extract
  1 (8-ounce) can crushed pineapple, undrained
  2 cups chopped bananas
  1 cup chopped pecans or walnuts

Frosting
  1 cup (2 sticks) butter, softened
  2 8-ounce packages of cream cheese, softened
  2 cups confectioners' sugar
  1 tablespoon lemon juice
  1 teaspoon vanilla extract

Preheat the oven to 350ºF (180ºC, Gas Mark 4). In a large bowl, whisk together the flour and next 4 ingredients; add the eggs and oil (or applesauce), stirring just until the dry ingredients are moistened. Stir in vanilla, pineapple, bananas, and 1 cup chopped toasted pecans. Spoon batter into 3 well-greased (with shortening) and floured 9-inch round cake pans.

Bake for 25-30 minutes or until a wooden toothpick inserted in center comes out clean. Cool cake layers in pans on wire racks 10 minutes; remove from pans to wire racks, and cool completely (about 1 hour).

Place one cake layer on a serving platter. Spread one cup of the cream cheese frosting over the cake layer. Top with the second layer and spread one cup of frosting over cake layer. Top with the third cake layer, and spread the top and sides of the cake with the remaining frosting. Arrange the toasted pecan halves in a circular pattern over the top of cake.

Frosting:

Beat the butter and cream cheese together with a hand-held electric mixer until smooth and creamy. Beat in the confectioners' sugar in increments. Lastly, beat in the lemon juice and vanilla.

Yield: 12 servings

IF YOU ENJOYED…

If you enjoyed *A FINAL GIFT*, please consider reviewing it on your favorite online review site. Thank you!

Find Lorraine online …
http:www.LorraineBartlett.com

AN UNEXPECTED VISITOR

A TALE FROM BLYTHE COVE MANOR

DESCRIPTION

AN UNEXPECTED VISITOR

All is quiet at Blythe Cove Manor as its proprietress, Blythe Calvert, anticipates a peaceful holiday along with her cat, Martha. But then a taxi pulls up and drops off a troubled, runaway teen looking for a safe haven. Can the magic of Blythe Cove Manor heal this young girl's aching heart?

A DARK AND STORMY NIGHT

The sun set way too early in December, and on that evening, the snow fell fast and furiously. At least that was the impression Blythe Calvert got as she looked out the big picture window that overlooked her sleeping gardens. It was the perfect Christmas weather—even if the holiday was still two days away. Of course, once she turned off the outside light, the wind-whipped flakes seemed to disappear into the wintery gloom.

Cupped in her hands was a mug of cocoa that she'd spiked with half a shot of peppermint schnapps. It would be a quiet holiday at Blythe Cove Manor. It wasn't that Blythe didn't want to spend the day with her extended family or friends, but it had been a hectic year, and more than anything she craved peace and quiet. Not that she didn't love taking care of her guests—she did. But she'd made a deliberate choice this year to have a few days before and after the holiday to be by herself and revel in solitude.

Of course, Martha's Vineyard in December wasn't exactly a destination spot. The cruel, raw wind off the ocean and the pelting snow were enough to make the toughest islanders long to hunker down before a blazing hearth. New Englanders were used to winter's blitz—especially those born on the island. The local cemetery was full of Calverts who'd lived and died on the island for over two hundred years. The house where she now stood was almost as old. It had been added onto over the generations and the main house now boasted a dozen guest rooms. It was a stretch for one woman to operate such an establishment, but with seasonal help, it was more than doable.

Blythe had given her most recent helper a nice holiday bonus, and the inn wasn't scheduled to reopen until February for Valentine's Day. That would give Blythe time to feel restored and plan for the boisterous summer to come.

She wandered into the living room and breathed in the scent of the ten-foot, spruce Christmas tree that decorated the southeast corner of the room. It held not only vintage family ornaments, but popcorn and cranberry garlands, as well as ornaments gifted by former patrons. It pleased Blythe to look at it.

In a basket filled with quilts that languished near the fireplace, Martha—Blythe Cove Manor's mascot tabby cat—slept in heavenly peace. Blythe walked past her kitty, giving her pet a skritch behind the ear and was rewarded with a sleepy *"Brrrp."*

Blythe ambled over to the TV. She'd set out a number of DVDs to choose from for her evening's entertainment, but it was still too early to even contemplate what she would watch. Among the titles were *White Christmas, Love Actually,* and *The Polar Express.*

Blythe smiled. She wasn't yet ready to make her decision. First, she would make some New England clam chowder, eat a couple of homemade rolls spread with a thick coating of sweet butter, and then hunker down on the couch with Martha on her lap to enjoy one of her favorite holiday movies. But there were still hours and hours to pass before that would happen.

So she picked up the remote for the stereo system, cranked up the sound, and enjoyed yet another carol from the five-disk CD player. Yes, it would have been pleasant to spend the holiday with friends or family, but she was also quite comfortable being alone with her cat.

Blythe settled in on the couch and sipped her cocoa, letting the holiday music saturate her soul like a sponge soaking up water. The warmth of the crackling fire was pleasant, and as she sipped the last of the chocolate, she reflected on Christmases past spent with her parents, her grandparents, aunts and uncles, and a myriad of cousins—far too many of whom had passed on during the years. While she mourned their loss, she also celebrated their lives and how they had enriched her own.

The wind seemed to pick up, howling even louder, but Blythe wasn't at all concerned. No matter what Mother Nature delivered, she knew the big gas-powered generator on the south side of the inn would keep her—and the old homestead—safe from the elements.

And so it was that she hunkered deeper into the reaches of the big leather couch, setting her feet on the old blanket chest that served as a coffee table, and felt every muscle in her body begin to relax. As she was about to give in to drowsiness, she felt a soft presence settle on her thighs and knew that Martha had decided to abandon her quilt haven for the warmth of her owner's lap.

All was right with the world, and nothing could spoil Blythe's serenity.

And then she heard the sound of a car engine outside the front of the manor, and seconds later, the sound of someone hammering on the front door.

"Sorry, Martha," Blythe said as she set her mug aside and lifted the cat off her lap, then got up to answer the door.

She looked through the peephole and saw Ed Thomas, a local taxi driver. *What in the world?*

Blythe threw open the door.

Ed stood before her, huddled into his worn corduroy jacket, a hunting cap with the ear flaps pulled down, and rubbing his hands for warmth. "Hey, Ed, what brings you out on a night like this?"

"I've got a customer for you."

"I'm closed," Blythe said firmly. "I won't reopen until Valentine's Day weekend. You know that."

"Yeah, well … the little lady didn't think ahead to make reservations. And," he said regretfully, "I suspect she hasn't got any money, which is why I didn't take her to the big inn in Edgartown. Truth is, I don't even know if she can pay me for bringing her out here."

"Little lady?" Blythe asked. "A child?"

"Not much more than. Maybe fourteen or fifteen. I think she might be a runaway. I figured if she was, that you might be the one who can best deal with her."

"There is the police station."

"Aw, Blythe—it's almost Christmas."

So it was.

There went Blythe's plans for a solitary holiday—or at least evening. And if the girl *was* a runaway, then what must her parents be thinking—wherever they were? Probably hoping that the girl ended up with a sympathetic individual who would take care of their precious daughter. Blythe had never walked away from a problem before; she wouldn't now.

She sighed. "Okay. Bring her in."

Ed nodded and went back to his vehicle. Blythe watched as he opened the back passenger side door, spoke to his charge, and then offered a hand to help her out of the back seat. The young girl wasn't dressed for the weather, wearing a light jacket inappropriate for December, a minuscule black skirt, tights, with her feet clad in black flats. She stood in the cold, waiting for Ed to grab her luggage from the back of his van. Then he toted it up to the front door, with her following behind.

"This here's Blythe Calvert. She owns Blythe Cove Manor." The girl said nothing, her brown eyes wide and scared. "You won't find a nicer place to stay on the island," Ed said.

The girl looked back at him. "Thank you."

The three of them looked at each other as the wind blew in the terrible cold air.

"What do you need, Ed?" Blythe asked.

"Not a damn thing, Blythe. Merry Christmas—and to you, too, little lady."

The young girl said nothing.

Ed gave a wave and headed back to his taxi. The girl and Blythe watched him return to his vehicle, then back out and drive down the dark drive.

"Come in before we both freeze," Blythe said. The girl grabbed the handle on her small suitcase and dragged it inside. Blythe closed the door and the two of them stood in the entry-way, looking at one another.

"You know my name; I guess it's time you told me yours."

"Shelby "

"Hi, Shelby. Do you have a last name?"

The girl shook her head.

The child wasn't going to make this easy.

Blythe forced a smile. "Welcome to Blythe Cove Manor."

"Did you name your hotel after yourself?" Shelby asked.

Blythe shook her head. "No. My parents named *me* after the cove."

"What's a cove?"

"A safe inlet from the sea."

"Is this a safe place?" Shelby asked, her voice wobbling.

"Yes, it is."

Shelby looked like she might want to cry. What was this poor little girl running away from?

"Can I take your coat?" Blythe asked.

Shelby shook her head. She looked chilled to the bone. "It's such a cold night. I just had a cup of cocoa to warm me up. But after opening the door, I think I might need another one. How about you?"

Shelby didn't answer; just nodded vigorously. Hungry, too, Blythe would bet.

"Come into the kitchen and keep me company while I make a fresh batch."

"Okay." Shelby grasped the handle of her small suitcase, pulling it behind her as she followed Blythe into the big country kitchen. She took in the pleasant space, her eyes widening. "What is *that*?" she asked, eyeing the massive, ivory AGA cooker.

"It's a stove. A cooker, actually. It's English. It's probably not like what you're used to seeing in a kitchen."

"No," Shelby said, her eyes wide, her voice a whisper.

"It's really very efficient...once you get a handle on how it works."

Shelby looked skeptical but said nothing. She watched in silence as Blythe measured the milk, cocoa powder, and sugar into a saucepan.

"Do you like cookies?" Blythe asked.

Shelby nodded, still looking like a loud noise might make her bolt for cover.

Blythe reached over to a covered plastic container, lifted the lid, and offered the girl a cut-out cookie. She'd made them earlier in the day, taking her time to decorate each and every one. Half of them were hearts covered in pink frosting, which she would freeze and bring out to guests during her Valentine's weekend. Shelby shook her head and Blythe replaced the canister.

"So, you're not from around here," Blythe said as she stirred the milky mixture.

"No," Shelby admitted.

"New to the island?"

"Sort of. I came here two years ago with my Aunt Alicia."

"It's a nice place to visit. And an even better place to live—if you can stand the winters," Blythe said rather blithely.

"We came in the summer," Shelby admitted. "But it was the best vacation I ever had. Well, it was the *only* vacation I ever had."

"So where do you hail from?" Blythe asked.

"Around," Shelby answered evasively.

"I was born right here on the island—like many generations of my family."

"Where *is* your family?" Shelby said, looking around. "You seem to be alone here."

"Yes, I am. And this year, it's by choice."

"How come?"

Blythe shrugged, still stirring the cocoa. "I needed some time on my own. Martha and me."

"Who's Martha?" Shelby asked, looking around as if expecting someone to jump out of the shadows.

"My cat. Didn't you see her when you came in?"

Shelby shook her head.

"Do you have any pets?"

"Rick has a pit bull. I'm afraid of it."

"Rick?" Blythe asked.

"My mother's boyfriend."

"What's the dog's name?"

"Dog."

"Really?"

"Yeah. Rick keeps him tied up outside most of the time. I tried to make friends with it, but it's too wild."

"And why's that?"

"Rick has him trained to fight."

Blythe's stomach did a flip-flop. "The poor thing."

"Yeah," Shelby said, her gaze fixed on the tile floor.

Bubbles began to form around the edges of the mixture. Blythe added the vanilla, stirred, and then took the pan off the hob. "Cocoa's ready. Reach up into that cupboard overhead and you'll find some mugs."

Shelby did as she was asked and came up with two matching mugs with cats on them. Blythe had bought them from a local potter several years before. The sight of one or both of them always made her smile.

She poured the cocoa into the mugs, settled a couple of green-frosted Christmas cookies onto a plate and set everything on a tray. "Come on. Let's take this into the living room."

Still pulling her small suitcase, Shelby followed Blythe past the tables in the dining area to the big couch and chest, where Blythe set down the tray. Thanks to the fire, the area was toasty warm, and finally Shelby unzipped her coat.

"Can I hang it up now?" Blythe asked.

Again, Shelby shook her head.

They sat down. Shelby made sure her case was situated beside her—in case she had to make a fast getaway? Blythe picked up a mug and a cookie and sat back. Shelby settled on the edge of the cushion farthest away from her hostess and looked around, as though assessing the threat of danger. What was the poor girl afraid of?

"A little later, I thought I might watch a movie. How would you like that?"

Shelby shrugged. Her gaze had focused on one of the cookies.

"They're good cookies," Blythe said. "I made them myself."

"The frozen kind you bake?"

Blythe shook her head. "No, from scratch."

"What does that mean?"

"I measured the flour, sugar, and other ingredients, then I rolled out the dough, used cookie cutters for the various shapes, and baked and frosted them."

"It seems like a lot of work for something that just gets eaten."

"I enjoy baking and cooking. Some people say that cooking is an expression of love."

"We eat McDonald's. It's cheap."

"I guess so," Blythe reluctantly agreed.

Shelby's gaze went once again to the cookie, and she quickly snatched it up, devouring it in two bites. Then she grabbed the mug of cocoa and drank it down in less than ten swallows. The kid must have been starving.

She set the mug back down and wriggled out of the sleeves of her jacket. This time, Blythe didn't ask to hang it up.

"So, is this some kind of hotel?" Shelby asked.

"It's a bed and breakfast. Some people call it an inn. Some people say that magical things happen here."

"There's no such thing as magic."

"Are you sure?" Blythe asked.

Shelby nodded, looking sadder still.

"I don't know about that. Why don't you go over there and look at the tree."

"What for?" Shelby asked.

"Just go and look at it. Maybe you'll find something on it that will surprise you."

Shelby frowned, but got up from her seat, leaving her jacket, but not her suitcase, behind.

Blythe sipped her cocoa, watching the girl as she circled the tree, examining every ornament until …

"Hey, what's this?" Shelby asked, turning to Blythe, confusion plastered across her young face.

"What's what?"

"This colored ball. It's got my name on it."

"Does it?" Blythe asked. She got up from the couch, leaving her mug on the blanket chest to join the girl. She bent down to examine the glass ornament. Sure enough, written in white flocked lettering was a vintage Christmas ornament that proclaimed in a neat script: SHELBY.

"When did you put this on the tree?"

"I don't remember putting it on the tree."

"Then how did it get there?" Shelby asked, sounding confused.

"I told you; some people think this is a magical place."

Shelby looked from Blythe back to the ornament and frowned, then she reached for her suitcase's handle, as though needing to seek comfort from something solid she could hold.

"We should think about where you're going to sleep tonight," Blythe said. She tapped her lips with her left index finger. "I know the perfect room. Follow me."

She started off across the living room's expanse, but paused when she got to the stairs. Shelby had not followed her. "Well, what are you waiting for?"

Shelby seemed to ponder that question for a moment, and then walked to the couch to retrieve her coat before pulling her suitcase to catch up with Blythe.

Blythe mounted the stairs to the second floor, and turned left at the landing. She paused before a door with a small painting attached to it. "This room is called Seaside. It's one of my favorites. I think you may like it."

She took a key from her slacks pocket and opened the door, stepping inside.

Shelby hung back, standing at the threshold, peeking inside.

Blythe stood beside the four-poster bed. "The bathroom is just through that door. Why don't you take a few minutes to get settled, and then you can come down and help me make supper."

"I don't know how to cook."

"Then now's a good time to learn," Blythe said brightly.

She waited until Shelby entered the room, heading for the bathroom, before leaving the room. "I'll see you in a few minutes, right?"

Shelby said nothing, still taking in her new accommodations.

Blythe didn't bother to close the door, but headed down the passageway and then the stairs, toward the kitchen, wondering how she would ever get Shelby to open up. Trust was an issue, and she had no doubt the girl had felt betrayed in the past.

She'd just have to rely on her instincts … but wondered what kind of child she was harboring, and what her legal obligations actually were. Not that she planned to turn the girl away, but she wasn't sure the law would look kindly on her taking in a runaway.

She'd just have to wait and see.

DINNER FOR TWO

Shelby looked around the pretty room with white furniture, pale blue walls, and pictures of roses decorating it. It was kind of corny, but it was welcoming. Almost everything in it was old, but well-cared-for, not unlike her Aunt Alicia's home in Connecticut. She'd been there on numerous occasions … usually when her mother was in court-ordered rehab. She'd never wanted to leave, but Jenny—she couldn't stand to be called *Mom*; she said it made her sound *old*—always convinced some do-gooder social worker that Shelby would be better off with her than any random person on the planet. And then when she had custody once again, they picked up and moved, sometimes even changing their names to stay one step ahead of Social Services.

But that life was now over. She had no intention of ever returning to live with Jenny.

Shelby took in the little, lighted Christmas tree that sat on top of the dresser. It was decorated in tiny crocheted white ornaments in the shape of stars and snowflakes. She'd learned how to crochet several years before while staying with her aunt. The elderly lady next door waited for her to get off the bus every day and Shelby would stay with her until her aunt got off work and came to collect her. Mrs. Peterson had taught her the craft and even given her a couple of crochet hooks and yarn, and she was just starting to get good at it when Jenny swooped in and grabbed her once again, hauling her off to a crummy, roach-infested apartment in South Boston. The hooks and yarn had been there the morning she'd started at yet another school, but they were gone when she got home that afternoon.

Home. What a farce.

Shelby walked into the bathroom and studied her pale face in the mirror over the sink. If she wore make-up, she was sure she could pass for sixteen—old enough to get a job—and maybe even eighteen. She pulled her mousy brown hair back. Yes, she would be able to pass for eighteen. Before she'd left the apartment in the wee hours that morning, she'd tiptoed into the darkened room that Jenny and Rick shared, grabbed several of her mother's outfits and stuffed them into her small case. They were a little baggy, but maybe if she washed them in hot water, she could shrink them. Her plan was to find a booming restaurant and work as a waitress.

She frowned, letting her hair fall back down around her shoulders. The taxi driver had said a lot of the businesses on the island were closed for the winter—including a lot of the restaurants. Maybe she should have gone to a big city instead of the sticks, but Shelby figured with miles of ocean between her and the mainland, it might be harder for the cops—or whoever looked for runaway kids—to find her.

Shelby's stomach growled loudly. Except for the cocoa and the cookie, she hadn't eaten a thing in almost twenty-four hours. This Blythe lady seemed pretty nice. Could she trust her? Shelby wasn't sure. For all she knew, she could be on the phone to the cops at that moment.

Shelby used the bathroom, washed her hands, and left the room, closing and locking the door behind her, then hurried down the stairs. The living room was empty, but Christmas music still issued from the stereo in the corner. Looking around, she noticed Blythe was indeed in the kitchen, standing in front of the counter. What was on the menu for dinner? Maybe in a fancy place like this, there'd be steak or roasted chicken. But when Shelby approached, she saw a plastic bag on the counter that boasted frozen clams.

Clams?

"What are you making?" Shelby asked.

"Clam chowder—New England style."

"Is there another kind?"

"Yes. This will be cream based. Manhattan clam chowder is made with tomatoes and other vegetables. Do you like chowder?"

"I only had it once. I don't think I liked it."

"Was it here on the island?"

"Uh-huh."

"Oh, then that surprises me. I've eaten the chowder at just about every restaurant on the island and I can't say I tasted a bad one yet. But I understand that if you're not used to it, then it might be an acquired taste," Blythe said, and began peeling a potato.

"What does that mean?"

"Tasting something you didn't like once, but giving it another chance and deciding to *try* to like it."

"That doesn't make sense."

Blythe smiled. "Maybe you'll feel differently when you're older."

"How much older?" Shelby asked.

"Maybe three or four years."

"How old do you think I am?"

Blythe paused in her peeling and scrutinized Shelby's face. "Thirteen."

"I'm nearly eighteen," Shelby asserted, sounding offended.

"Then you carry age well," Blythe said cheerfully. "Would you like to help me make the soup?"

Shelby shrugged. "I guess."

"What would you rather do: chop an onion or celery?"

"Onions make you cry," Shelby said suspiciously.

"Yes, sometimes they do. There's nothing wrong with a good cry once in a while."

"Only babies cry," Shelby lamented.

"I've been known to cry now and then, and I'm not a baby," Blythe said, handing Shelby a cutting board, a knife, and two ribs of celery.

"Why would you cry?"

"At the loss of a friend or a relative."

"People you love?" Shelby asked, and started slicing the celery. If she was honest, there was only one person she was fond of, and it wasn't her mother.

Blythe added a hunk of butter to a saucepan on the cooker. "Uh-huh."

"When else?"

Blythe laughed. "When I watch sad—or even happy movies."

"How can something happy make you cry?"

"When it touches you inside. Gives you empathy. Sometimes it even brings you joy."

"What kind of things?" Shelby pressed. She'd never been happy enough to cry. In her almost fourteen years, she'd rarely *been* happy.

"Well, Christmas movies. I've got a stack of them in the living room. I was planning to watch a bunch of them over the next couple of days. Many of them have wonderful endings that are so sweet they make me cry."

"Which ones?"

"Oh, the ending of *Love Actually*. People at Heathrow Airport all hugging loved ones they hadn't seen in a while. It's very powerful."

"I never heard of that movie."

"I think you might like it."

Why would she think that? Shelby had felt tremendous relief —although maybe not love—during the times her Aunt Alicia had taken her to stay with her in Connecticut. Shelby had once stayed for as long as a year, but sometimes only for days at a time, but they had been the happiest days of her life.

Some of the kids at school whined and cried when their parents had separated or divorced; but if she could have wrangled it, Shelby would have happily divorced herself from her addict mother. She'd had to take care of the woman when they lived alone, and she'd had to watch out for herself when Jenny had shacked up with a pimp or a drug dealer. The men her mother chose were rarely kind, and were more often brutal—not only to Jenny, but their pets, as well. Like Rick and Dog. Shelby had learned to survive by keeping a low profile at school and especially at whatever place she'd been forced to call home.

Blythe finished chopping the onion and tossed it into the pot, where it immediately began to sizzle. "How's that celery coming along?"

"All chopped," Shelby said.

Blythe scooped up the celery pieces and added them to the pot. "Would you like to watch this while I get everything else ready?"

"Sure." Shelby stepped up to the stove, accepting the wooden spoon as though it was a baton in a relay race. She stirred the onions and celery around the pot before looking askance at Blythe, who measured the rest of the ingredients. It had never occurred to Shelby that cooking might be enjoyable. Her mother usually just tossed a fast-food bag at her. When she'd been with her aunt, she never thought to ask her if she might help with dinner prep. Why hadn't her aunt asked her to help?

A lump rose in Shelby's throat.

Maybe her aunt had never asked her to help because when

she'd tried to hug Shelby, the girl had pulled away. Shelby saw her friends' mothers kiss and tease them. Was Aunt Alicia *afraid* to do that because the walls around Shelby's heart had forced her aunt to keep her distance?

Maybe.

Two weeks before, Shelby had spent a weekend at Adriana Ryan's home. Adriana lived in a beautiful townhouse. Her parents were nice. Even her little brother was okay. You could tell when you walked into that place that none of them were hiding secrets. None of them had to.

It felt really bad to have to hide a big part of your life from everyone around you. But as Shelby stirred the onions and celery, she had to admit that though she'd only been in Blythe's home for less than an hour, and barely knew the woman who stood only two feet from her, for some reason she felt safe here. But how long would Blythe let her stay? Could she really find a job? How long would it take for her to make enough money to find a place to live? Was it realistic to think a girl of thirteen could actually pull off such an enormous task? But what were her options? Stay and starve, or go back to Jenny's apartment and become rape bait? Of the two options, she preferred the former.

"It's time to put everything together and make the soup," Blythe said. Shelby moved aside to let her benefactor take over. She watched with interest as Blythe added the rest of the ingredients to the pan. And while she wasn't sure she would like clam soup, Shelby had to admit the concoction smelled pretty good.

"How long does it have to cook?" Shelby asked.

"Until the potatoes are soft. About ten minutes."

"Can I stir it?"

"Of course you can," Blythe said, handing back the wooden spoon.

Again, Shelby stepped up to stand before the big ivory AGA and stirred and stirred the soup. When she looked up, she found Blythe watching her and smiling.

Shelby smiled back. It felt odd, but good, to smile. She'd had so little to smile about during her life. Escaping to Martha's Vineyard had been the right decision. The taxi driver bringing her to this quiet, beautiful home with a sympathetic owner had been a tremendous stroke of luck.

Maybe—just maybe—Shelby's life was about to change for the better.

BLYTHE RETRIEVED the antique tureen from the cupboard and set it on the counter. It had belonged to her great-great-grandmother and had served not only family members, but hundreds of guests as well.

Blythe had already set one of the tables in the B&B's dining room with her best china, wanting her guest to feel welcome and relaxed in her home.

"Supper's ready," Blythe called, carrying the tureen into the dining room. A plate heaped with rolls already awaited them, along with a dish of sweet whipped butter. The wind howled outside, but inside all was cozy.

Shelby tore herself away from the twinkling Christmas tree lights and approached the table.

"Sit down," Blythe encouraged, and picked up the silver ladle, dipping it into the tureen and doling out the chowder to the bowl on the opposite side of the table.

"Not so much—in case I don't like it," Shelby said. "I don't want to waste it."

Blythe nodded, then filled her own bowl. She had no qualms when it came to New England clam chowder.

She sat down, picked up a roll, and set it on the small plate before her, then passed it to Shelby. In silence, they buttered their rolls and Blythe picked up her spoon to take a taste of the chowder. She watched with interest as Shelby picked up her own spoon with what seemed like trepidation, but then tried the soup. She didn't shudder or grimace, and took another taste.

"This is pretty good."

"Most home-cooked meals are," Blythe said, spooning up another mouthful. They ate in silence for more than a minute, but there were questions that needed answering and Blythe was determined to ask them. Gently.

"Did you like the time you spent here on the island on your first visit?"

Shelby tore off a piece of her roll and spread a thick layer of butter on it. "Sure. It was really nice."

"Where did you stay on the island?"

Shelby shrugged. "Just some little motel."

"Was it nice?"

Again she shrugged. "It had a kitchenette. We saved money on breakfast and dinner because of the fridge and microwave. But we always had lunch out—because lunch is cheaper than dinner in a restaurant."

Blythe nodded. "Did you visit Edgartown and Vineyard Haven?"

"I guess."

"What did you enjoy best about the island?"

"One night we went to see a bunch of old houses with paper lanterns all lit up."

"That's what we call Illumination Night. It's a yearly event and draws thousands of people."

"It sure was crowded," Shelby agreed, "but the lights were so pretty. My aunt really liked them. She bought some of those lanterns and hung them on her porch." The girl lapsed into silence for a few moments, as though lost in thought. Then she shook herself. "What do you do for fun around here?"

"The island is a destination for a lot of people, but for me, it's just my home. I spend my summers working here at the manor and gardening."

"It doesn't sound like much fun," Shelby groused.

"It depends on your definition of fun. I enjoy hosting guests. I get to meet all kinds of people from all walks of life and never have to leave my home. I get to cook for them, which brings me enormous satisfaction." Blythe ate more of her soup. "What are your plans? Are you just visiting, or are you planning an extended stay?"

"I was thinking I might stay. But first I have to get a job."

"Hmm." Blythe shook her head. "That might be tough at this time of year. We're a seasonal destination. There aren't many businesses that stay open year-round. What were you planning to do?"

Just what the taxi driver had said.

"Waitress. Maybe be a bartender. I heard bartenders make a lot of money."

"Parts of the island are dry."

Shelby frowned. "What does that mean?"

"That they don't serve alcohol. People bring their own liquor, so there aren't as many opportunities for being a bartender as you might think."

Shelby's frown deepened. "Oh."

"Where do you plan to live?"

"I thought I'd rent a little house near the beach," Shelby said nonchalantly.

"In what town?"

"Um … the big one."

"Edgartown?"

"Yeah."

"Pretty pricy," Blythe said offhandedly.

"Then … maybe one of the smaller ones."

"A lot of rentals are also seasonal. They weren't built to be used in our brutal winters."

"Really?"

Blythe nodded.

Shelby dipped her spoon into her chowder more slowly.

"Have you got enough money saved for first and last month's rent?" Blythe asked.

"What does that mean?"

"A lot of apartments and houses for rent require you to put up enough money to pay for the first month you rent, as well as the last month. And many also want a security deposit for at least another month's rent."

"That's a lot of money," Shelby said quietly, setting her spoon down. Her face had paled once again.

Blythe picked up the ladle and added more chowder to her bowl. "Yes, it is."

"Do you require that kind of upfront money?"

"My guests usually only stay for a few days or a week, but yes —I require a deposit, too. That's just the way a business is run."

Shelby's head dipped. "I guess I have a lot to learn about that kind of stuff."

"Were you thinking of going into hotel management or anything of the kind?"

"I—I don't think I know what that is."

"There're colleges that have programs where you can learn all about how to run a hotel or a small inn. I went to Cornell University for my degree. I learned a lot, and it was a big help when I took over Blythe Cove Manor."

"How did you pay for college?"

"My parents helped me, but I also worked the entire time I was in school."

"What kind of job?"

Blythe smiled. "I cleaned rooms in one of the local hotels." She laughed. "After all these years, I'm *still* cleaning rooms."

Shelby looked horror-struck. "Even toilets?"

"I'm afraid so," Blythe admitted wryly.

Shelby looked like she might want to cry.

"Is everything okay?" Blythe asked.

Shelby nodded, but Blythe suspected the girl had just received a staggering look at reality.

"Would you like more chowder?" Blythe asked.

Shelby shook her head.

Blythe finished her soup and roll before she stood. "Why don't you head into the living room and choose a movie for us to watch while I take care of these dishes."

Shelby nodded. "Okay."

Blythe cleared the table and put the leftover soup in a plastic container in the fridge, and stowed the leftover rolls in a bag. They might well end up in the stuffing for the chicken she intended to roast for her Christmas dinner.

By the time she returned to the living room, Martha had reappeared and sat on the back of the couch, while Shelby had queued up the movie.

"What are we going to watch?"

"I wanted to see that movie with the airport stuff you mentioned."

Love Actually.

"Good choice. It's one of my favorites."

Blythe turned off the stereo and let Shelby take command of the TV and DVR remotes. She pushed play, and the movie began.

It must have been a very long day for Shelby, for within five minutes of the start of the movie the girl had snuggled into the corner of the couch and was fast asleep. It was time for Blythe to do a little research.

Easing off the sofa, she tiptoed away, heading to her computer to begin her research.

First off, by Shelby's description, Blythe was pretty sure she knew which motel the girl and her aunt had stayed at during their vacation two years previously. And while she didn't have the aunt's—or Shelby's—last name, she did have the aunt's first name and could narrow down when they'd stayed on the island; during the Illumination two years previously—the exact date was only a Google search away. She knew Burt Matthews, the owner of the motel, thanks to their Chamber of Commerce affiliation, and fired off an email giving him a brief explanation as to why she needed the information. As it was so close to Christmas, she wasn't sure when—or even *if*—she'd get an answer. If she didn't hear from him in a couple of days, she would call—and hope that he hadn't gone south for the winter.

In the meantime, what was she supposed to do with a runaway girl? A girl who may or may not have been reported as missing. Blythe didn't dislike the kid, but she certainly couldn't keep her indefinitely, either.

What would make a child run away from home, anyway? For some reason, Blythe was sure that in this case, Shelby hadn't had a frivolous reason to seek a safe refuge. She must have felt secure with her aunt and here on the island. Had her time here represented a haven from her regular life? And how did this aunt figure into her life? The way Shelby had spoken about the woman, Blythe reckoned that Shelby had a good relationship with the woman. By process of elimination, did that mean she didn't have a good rapport with her parent or parents? She'd mentioned Rick and a dog. That sounded like she lived with her mother and a boyfriend—and that it wasn't a pleasant arrangement.

Blythe sat back and pondered the situation. She'd led what she liked to think of as a charmed life—in more ways than one. She had a lovely home. She had a job that allowed her to meet wonderful, gracious people who she enjoyed entertaining and it was her pleasure to serve. There was so much trouble in the world, most of which she didn't encounter on a daily basis. But she had a feeling Shelby had had more than a lifetime's worth of unhappiness and disappointment during her short time on the planet. Blythe felt that the key to the girl's happiness was probably her aunt—but what could the woman do if she couldn't wrest custody of the girl? Perhaps she'd offer her asylum during the time when Shelby's mother either abandoned her or just didn't care enough.

The sad fact was that the Social Services' goal of keeping families together wasn't always in the best interest of the child. Sometimes parents weren't the greatest role models and were ill-equipped to take care of the offspring they produced. Would turning Shelby in to the authorities just condemn her to a continued hellish life?

It was a sobering thought.

The computer pinged, and Blythe checked her email. Aha! Burt Matthews had replied to her note.

Will have to do some digging to find out what you need to know. Hope to have some info for you by the morning. Let me know if I can do anything else to help.

Blythe smiled, feeling grateful that, like her, her colleague had a soft heart. Still, would that be enough to give this fractured girl a Merry Christmas?

That was a question Blythe wasn't sure she could answer, but one she fully intended to try.

"SHELBY! SHELBY!"

Someone was shaking her shoulder, and Shelby cracked open an eye to see a woman standing over her. Oh, yes—Blythe. The innkeeper who had taken her in.

"It's almost eleven o'clock—it's time for bed. You slept through almost the entire movie."

Shelby rubbed at her eyes. "I'm sorry."

"Would you like me to walk you back to your room, or do you think you can find it on your own?"

"I'm not stupid," Shelby said irritably, sat up, and felt instantly sorry for her outburst.

"No problem," Blythe said. "If you need anything during the

night, just pick up the bedside phone and hit the pound key and four on the keypad. That will ring me directly. Okay?"

Shelby nodded. She felt like she ought to say something. Maybe thank the woman who had taken her in, but she wasn't sure how that might go over, so she kept silent.

"I'm usually up pretty early, so as soon as you're ready, come down for breakfast. I'm sure I can rustle up something we'd both enjoy. Do you like muffins or eggs for breakfast?"

"Eggs."

"How do you like them cooked?"

The only times Shelby had had a cooked breakfast was when she'd stayed with her Aunt Alicia. "Poached. On buttered toast. Soldiers, my aunt calls them." Her aunt had cut the toast into strips so that she could dip them into the wonderful runny yolks.

"One or two?"

"I could have two?" Shelby asked.

"You can have as many as you like," Blythe said.

"Two would be good," Shelby said.

Blythe nodded. "Then I'll say goodnight and see you bright and early in the morning."

Early? Maybe, maybe not.

Shelby rose from the couch and headed toward the staircase.

"Good night!" Blythe called.

"Yeah," Shelby said, although as soon as the word was out of her mouth she felt like she should have said something—anything—else.

Shelby climbed the stairs, heading for her room in the empty inn. It felt kind of creepy walking down the long, quiet corridor, and suddenly she felt terribly lonely. She had never been so far away from her regular life—no matter how crappy it was. But at least here she felt kind of safe. Not as safe as she'd be in Connecticut with her Aunt Alicia, but safe enough.

She'd made a conscious decision not to run to Connecticut. If Jenny decided to pursue her—never a given—that would be the first place she'd look. Jenny never had a kind word for Aunt Alicia—unless she wanted to dump Shelby on her. And then—on a whim—would change her mind. Maybe at some time in the future, Shelby could contact her aunt and let her know that she was okay, but that wouldn't happen until she got a job and found her own place to live. Would Blythe let her stay for a while? Maybe she could do something to stay in her good graces. Maybe clean the inn's rooms—but not the toilets—or shovel the driveway; anything that would keep her in a safe, warm place until she could pay for her own way—find her own place in this rotten, shitty, stinking world.

But Shelby also knew from bitter experience that goodwill only lasted so long. She needed to have an exit strategy. She needed to have a plan for her future.

But right then she was so tired, all she wanted to do was sleep. In a safe place. In a place where she wouldn't be molested or mauled by a dog whose life was even more miserable than her own.

The future was a dark, empty abyss.

Shelby entered the pretty room Blythe had given her. She locked the door behind her, which felt good. She wished she'd had that option back at the apartment she'd shared with Jenny and Rick.

She grabbed a sleep shirt from her suitcase and headed for the bathroom, which also had a lock on the door. She used it, too. The bathroom had a shower *and* a soaker tub. She could use either of them and not have to worry that someone would barge in on her—not with a lock on the room's door. She hadn't had a shower in weeks because of that fear. She turned on the shower's water to let it get hot, and then stripped off her clothes and stepped inside. Little bottles of shampoo and conditioner sat on a shelf, as well as a brand-new cake of sweet-smelling soap. Shelby stood under the spray and let its warmth seep into not only her body but her soul.

She'd made it this far. She might have a day—maybe two—before she was going to be forced to seriously think about her future. But because of the holiday, she also figured she might be able to prevail on Blythe's goodwill for a couple of days before she'd have to make some decisions.

As she toweled off and donned her sleep shirt, Shelby realized she was too sleepy to think about what she needed to do next.

It could wait until tomorrow … or the next day.

Turning off the bathroom light, Shelby was grateful that the pretty little Christmas tree on the dresser acted as a nightlight. Jenny had never erected a Christmas tree. Some years there was a present—something Jenny had received from a charity to give to Shelby—and there had always been a package from Aunt Alicia, but Shelby had never experienced a TV Christmas. One where people cared about each other, gave presents to each other that didn't get left behind after a hasty move to an even crummier apartment or a homeless shelter.

As she climbed under the bed's luxurious covers, pulling them up to her neck, Shelby felt a peace she'd seldom experienced and wished she could call her aunt. For she was sure that in this whole wide world only one person really cared about her … and that person wasn't her mother.

Shelby grabbed the extra pillow from the other side of the bed and hugged it. After a while, it felt warm—reflecting her body heat—and was soft like the ones in Aunt Alicia's guest room. She'd felt safe there, too.

The memory of that pretty room made her happy and sad at the same time, just like Blythe had described earlier. So happy—and sad—that tears leaked from her eyes. And it was with a heavy heart that she cried herself to sleep.

HAPPY HOLLANDAISE

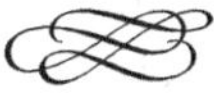

*B*lythe was up early that Christmas Eve morning. The first thing she did after feeding her cat was to check her email and was delighted to see that the owner of the Ocean-view Motel had sent her a note.

Couldn't sleep thinking about your young guest, so I searched our files and I think may have found the information you might need.

Blythe studied the note. Not only was there a full name and address for Shelby's aunt, but a phone number, email, and snail mail address, too.

She waited until eight o'clock to call, and was relieved when the call was answered. Sadly, she learned more than she really wanted to know, but was also given a promise that Shelby's aunt would make the drive to come and retrieve the girl later in the day. Blythe extended an invitation for them to stay for Christmas, but wasn't surprised when Alicia McKendrick didn't give her a yay or nay. Understandably, there were just too many extenuating circumstances for her to make a commitment. Still, Blythe urged the woman to pack a bag—just in case.

No sooner had she hung up the phone, than Shelby appeared in her kitchen, all tousled-haired and sleepy-eyed.

"Ready for breakfast?" Blythe asked cheerfully.

Shelby nodded. Still clad in a long T-shirt, the girl sidled up to the counter, leaning against it as if she might keel over without its support.

"What would you like: coffee, tea, or cocoa?"

"Cocoa sounds good."

"Cocoa it is," Blythe said, and turned to the industrial-sized fridge to grab the gallon-sized jug of milk. She poured a reasonable quantity into a saucepan and set it on the cooker's boiling plate, then turned for the pantry to grab the cocoa and sugar.

"Still crave those poached eggs?"

Shelby nodded. "That would be nice."

In the background, the local radio station played non-stop Christmas music. Blythe reached over to turn up the sound. She wrinkled her nose.

"What's that I smell?" Shelby asked.

"Hollandaise sauce. Many of my guests have complimented me on it. It's made of eggs, a little lemon juice, and butter."

Shelby noticed a saucepan of water sat on the cooker, bubbling away. "What's that for?"

"Your poached eggs."

"I don't get it."

"Poaching means to cook food in a water bath."

"So you're going to be putting egg sauce on eggs?"

"That's right.

"There're English muffins on the counter. Take out a couple, slice them, and pop them in the toaster. While you do that, I'll see to the eggs," Blythe said.

Shelby did as she was told, but then turned to watch as Blythe cracked an egg into a small bowl. She picked up a bottle of white vinegar, opened the cap, and poured a small amount into the boiling water. Then she grabbed a spoon and started stirring the water until she had a mini whirlpool going. She dumped the egg into the water, and Shelby watched as the white wrapped around the yoke until it looked like a big white blob.

"Where did you learn to make eggs that way?" Shelby asked.

"My mother. She taught me a lot about cooking. It's served me well over the years."

Shelby scowled. "My mother never taught me a damn thing."

"Oh?" Blythe asked, cracking another egg into the small dish. "Are you sure?"

Shelby nodded. "She was always too preoccupied."

"In what way?"

"She's into drugs. She's…she's an addict."

"Oh, I'm so sorry," Blythe said. But Shelby wasn't sure if Blythe was sorry for Jenny or her. She shrugged. "I learned in school that if you have an addict for a parent, you might be an addict, too."

"I guess that depends on the decisions you make."

"What do you mean?"

"Well, if you see how drugs can destroy a life, you might want to avoid them at all costs."

"But what if I'm just as weak as her?" Shelby asked, and had to acknowledge that that fact had preyed on her mind far too often.

"It's possible. You know—it's Christmas Eve. Why don't we think some happier thoughts?" Blythe suggested.

"You mean like happily ever after?" Shelby asked snidely.

"Sometimes it happens, but more often we have to work hard to find happiness."

Shelby looked around the pretty kitchen. "I'll bet you've never been unhappy a day in your life."

"You'd be surprised," Blythe said somberly. She wasn't about to elaborate. She scooped the first egg out of the water, letting it drain while Shelby buttered the muffin halves. Blythe stirred the water once more before dropping the second egg in.

"Christmas isn't such a big deal," Shelby said blandly. "It's really just another day on the calendar."

"You think so?" Blythe asked.

"Sure."

Blythe gazed heavenward. "It wasn't when I was a girl. We had wonderful Christmases. If the weather was fine, we would go down and walk on the beach. If it was stormy, we would huddle in front of the fireplace and my relatives would tell stories about the past. There'd be a wonderful big dinner and lots of presents."

Shelby looked around the kitchen and into the big empty dining room beyond. "You're here all alone."

Blythe nodded. "Yes, I've lost most of my family, who either died or moved away. But I have memories of wonderful Christmases past that I can relive over and over again. It's a comfort."

Blythe captured the second egg from the swirling waters, let it drain, then set it and the other on the waiting plate and topped them with sauce. "Go ahead and take yours into the dining room. I'll follow as soon as mine is ready. And don't wait for me. Eat your breakfast while it's hot."

"Okay," Shelby said, taking her food into the next room. By the time Blythe joined her with her breakfast, Shelby had already devoured her own.

"Did you have enough?"

"Yeah," Shelby said, smiling. "It was *really* good."

Blythe picked up her fork. "I'd already planned my day before you arrived."

Shelby's expression darkened, and for a moment she seemed to cower like a frightened dog expecting a blow.

"I'd planned to bake some cookies and make fudge. Would you like to help me with that?"

For a moment, Shelby's expression was blank, but then she seemed to shake herself. "Fudge?"

"Yes. My favorite is peanut butter. What's yours?"

"I love peanut butter, too."

"Then we're agreed," Blythe said and lifted her fork to her mouth to enjoy the first taste of that lovely poached egg.

"What kind of cookies were you planning to make?" Shelby asked.

"I hadn't made up my mind. I've already made cut-outs, and though I like them, they aren't my favorites."

"What are?" Shelby asked.

"It's a tossup. Either chocolate chip or butterscotch oatmeal cookies. How about you?"

Shelby ducked her head, looking sheepish. "I don't know. I haven't eaten a lot of homemade cookies. Jenny usually buys them by the bags at the grocery store. She likes Oreos."

"Have you ever had shortbread?" Blythe asked.

Shelby wrinkled her nose. "Small loaves of bread?"

Blythe smiled. "No. Butter cookies."

"I've never had them before."

"Then that's what we'll make, because they are *wonderful*."

"Sounds okay to me," Shelby agreed. "And you'll let me help make them?"

"Of course. It'll be much more fun to share the experience. But I will have to do some paperwork today."

"Even if you're not open?" Shelby asked.

Blythe nodded. "You'd be surprised how much activity goes on behind the scenes, even when my B&B isn't open to the public."

Shelby nodded, as though she understood—but Blythe was pretty sure the girl had no idea what she was talking about.

'I've got some wonderful cookbooks. Maybe you'd like to look through them and pick out another recipe you'd like to make."

"I could do that?" Shelby asked, as though she'd never been given such a choice.

"Of course."

"What if you don't have the ingredients to make them?"

"The local grocery store is open until four this afternoon. If I don't have it, we could always go and get what we need."

"Does it have to be an *official* Christmas cookie recipe?" Shelby asked.

"Not at all. What's your favorite cookie?"

Shelby's brow furrowed as she pondered her reply. "Once, at school, one of the kids' mothers brought in some kind of painted cookie. Lila said they made them and they had to dry and then they painted them."

Blythe nodded. "I know what you mean. They're called Springerle, and they're sort of like a cut-out cookie, only they're made with a wooden mold. I have several of them in different designs."

Shelby's shoulders slumped.

"But that doesn't mean we can't *try* to make them. I think it would be fun. What do you think?"

Shelby perked up. "I'd like to try."

"Then that's what we'll do."

A sound emitted from the computer behind the reception desk across the way.

Blythe forked up the last of her eggs and toast, chewed and swallowed. Then she set down her fork. "I need to check that email. I've been conversing with a couple who want to book a room for Valentine's Day. I'd better go check it."

Shelby nodded disinterestedly, and Blythe got up and headed for her computer at the reception desk. She tapped the keyboard, and the screen came to life. She read the latest e-mail message from Shelby's aunt and frowned. It was not good news, but in a way it might change the young girl's life for the better.

With a heavy heart, she typed a response and hit SEND.

It would be a long day, and during the long hours she would have to muster her best acting skills because she had a feeling what was to come might break Shelby's heart.

Blythe looked back to her charge. Shelby's gaze was focused on the twinkling Christmas tree. Was she actually smiling?

Then Blythe knew what her goal for the day had to be. To *keep* Shelby smiling.

"Hey, kiddo," she called. "Ready to start looking for cookie recipes?"

A SECOND VISITOR

Shelby and Blythe spent the bulk of the day in the manor's kitchen, cooking and baking. They'd made six batches of cookies, made the basis of their homemade pizza dinner, with Blythe letting Shelby knead the dough—and were at last making the fudge that Blythe had promised many hours before.

It seemed like Blythe had a million recipes stuffed into her brain. Still, for Shelby's sake, she would pull a book off a shelf so that she could follow along as they made each delicacy.

"I thought you had to cook fudge," Shelby said as they measured the ingredients into a microwaveable bowl.

"The first time I made fudge, I didn't have a candy thermometer. I decided to wing it. I figured I had been pretty successful in the kitchen, and what was the big deal about getting the mixture to a certain temperature anyway. Well, I learned my lesson. I didn't cook the mixture long enough and when it came time to eat the fudge, it tasted like chocolate sand."

Shelby wrinkled her nose. "I wouldn't like that."

"No, and neither did my family. I tried to bluff my way through it, but I think I only ate two pieces before I had to admit defeat. We threw the rest of it out. But making fudge with confectioners' sugar solves that problem. I've been making fudge in the microwave ever since and have never had a bad batch."

"Yet?" Shelby teased.

"Yet," Blythe admitted with a smile.

They set the bowl in the microwave and pushed the start button to melt the chocolate.

"Wow," Shelby said, looking out the window over the sink. Earlier in the day, she could see the ocean, but now the sky was a charcoal gray. "It sure gets dark here early."

"Yes it does, but now that we've passed the winter solstice, it's already getting brighter by a minute or two every day. By February, I always start to feel hopeful that spring will be right around the corner."

Looking forward to the future was way too scary to contemplate. Shelby was quite fine with putting off having to think about what she would do in the following days. But she also knew she could not expect the kind woman who owned this bed and breakfast to keep her indefinitely. She understood that the room she'd been given was meant for paying customers ... boy oh, how she liked that room. It was fit for a princess. She'd never slept on such a comfortable bed. When she ran the hot water, it came out of the tap steaming. The sample-size soap, shampoo, and conditioner all smelled like some kind of beautiful flower. Though she hadn't worn it, Shelby had found a fluffy, white terrycloth robe in the closet that was as soft as a kitten's fur. When she'd awoken during the night, the light from that special little Christmas tree had been comforting, making her feel safer than she had for a long, long time.

How soon would that feeling of safety be yanked from her?

Shelby glanced down at the recipe Blythe had provided. "It says here to line the pan with foil."

"I'll show you a little trick," Blythe said and tore a piece of aluminum from the roll. "You shape it around the outside of the pan first, like so—" Shelby watched with interest. "And then you place it inside the pan. It's nearly a perfect fit."

Shelby nodded. Was there nothing Blythe didn't know about cooking—and maybe life?

The microwave went off, and Blythe handed Shelby a spoon. "Go ahead and stir it, then we'll give it another two minutes." She did and then reset the microwave. She watched as the bowl went around and around in the little oven, while Blythe greased the lined pan with butter. When the microwave went *beep*, Blythe handed Shelby a couple of potholders and she picked up the pot. They added the confectioners' sugar and vanilla, stirring until it thickened.

"Now we've got to transfer the fudge into the prepared pan," Blythe instructed.

Shelby did so, then she held the bowl so that Blythe could scrape down the sides with a silicone spatula and spread it evenly in the pan. "Now what?"

"We put it in the fridge to firm up."

"When can we have a piece?"

"In an hour or so. But something that rich might spoil our pizza dinner."

Shelby looked over at the big bowl farther down the counter where the dough had been rising.

"When will we start the pizza?"

"In a little while. First, we have to decide what to have on the pizza. I'm a veggie girl, myself, but I do have some pepperoni we could slice."

"Vegetables on pizza?" Shelby asked. She'd never had anything other than slices of cheese and pepperoni pizzas—it was all Jenny ever ordered.

"Sure. I like onions, peppers, and broccoli can be really good."

"Broccoli?" Shelby repeated in horror. "That sounds disgusting."

Blythe laughed. "It's not—honestly. But, like clam chowder, it might be an acquired taste."

"When will we start making it?"

"You're not really hungry right now, are you?"

Shelby thought about the four cookies she'd had not an hour before. And the big lunch of chicken salad on a flaky croissant. While the croissants had been thawed, and Blythe had poached the chicken—not unlike the eggs earlier that day—to make the salad, adding nuts, raisins, and an apple. It had tasted *wonderful*.

"I guess I could wait a while," Shelby said. At home, she'd never known when a meal was likely to happen—if it ever did. There'd been days when there was nothing to eat in the apartment—usually on weekends. She got a free breakfast and lunch at school during the week. Weekends could be pretty bleak and she'd gotten used to going to bed hungry.

The sound of the wind picked up and Blythe moved from the kitchen to the big picture window in the dining area. She turned on the outside light and the snow swirled around it blowing every which way.

"Not a fit night out for man nor beast," Blythe said, clasping her arms as though cold, and yet it was comfortably warm in the big house.

Blythe switched out the light. "What do you want to do; watch part of a movie, take a break to put the pizza in the oven, and then watch the rest of it?"

"That sounds okay to me," Shelby said. She turned toward the living room and heard the sound of a car engine outside the inn. "Are you expecting company tonight?"

Blythe's expression darkened. "As a matter of fact, I am."

"Who?"

The engine died and a few seconds later someone rapped on the front door. Blythe left the kitchen and crossed the dining and living rooms, heading for the front door. Curious, Shelby followed.

Blythe grasped the door handle to answer it. "Won't you come in?" she invited, letting in a blast of cold air.

Shelby blinked, unable to believe her eyes. "Aunt Alicia?"

Bundled up in a parka, knit cap, and a scarf, the woman bounded forward, practically running to greet her niece, pulling her into a fierce hug.

"Oh, baby—you don't know how worried I've been."

Shelby stood stiffly in her aunt's embrace, her gaze shifting to Blythe, standing by the now-closed door, a hot flush of betrayal rushing through her.

"How did you find me?"

Aunt Alicia removed her hat and unwound her scarf. "I didn't find you; Blythe found *me*."

Shelby battled the growing hurt within her. But then, this wasn't the first time she'd been turned in—and it might not be the last. She looked around, but Blythe seemed to have disappeared. She looked toward the kitchen, but didn't see her there, either.

Aunt Alicia unzipped her coat. She grabbed Shelby's arm, pulling her over to the big leather couch. They both sat down, and Aunt Alicia shrugged off her coat, laying it over the arm of the sofa.

"I think you owe me an explanation. Why did you run away—and why here?"

Shelby couldn't look her aunt in the eye.

"What was wrong at home?" Aunt Alicia asked, her voice soft.

Shelby took in a long shuddering breath, sure she was about to cry.

"It's okay, honey. You know you can tell me anything."

"Rick," Shelby managed, her voice shaking.

Aunt Alicia let out a breath, almost as though she'd expected the answer. "Did he do something bad to you?"

Shelby focused her gaze on the hardwood floor. "Well … no.

Well, maybe. He … he grabbed me and … he touched me where he shouldn't—and more than once."

Aunt Alicia patted her hand, but Shelby pulled it back, wrapping her arms around herself.

"Why didn't you call me? Why didn't you come to me?" Aunt Alicia asked gently.

It took long moments before Shelby trusted her voice to stay steady enough to speak. "It didn't seem fair. I'm almost an adult. I should be able to take care of myself."

"So you came here—to Martha's Vineyard? What was your plan?"

"To hide out. To get a job. To take care of myself."

"Don't take this the wrong way," Aunt Alicia began, "but … you're not almost a grownup. Sweetheart, according to the law you are a child. You'll legally *remain* a child for another five years." Again, she touched Shelby, this time resting her hand on the girl's shoulder. "I know it doesn't seem fair, but those are the rules. They were made to protect kids like you from people like Rick. Do you understand?"

Shelby shrugged, still unwilling to face her aunt.

"If it's any consolation, you won't have to worry about Rick ever again."

At that piece of news, Shelby twisted to face her aunt. "Did he leave Jenny?"

Aunt Alicia looked distinctly unhappy. "In a manner of speaking." Shelby studied her aunt's face. She seemed to be wrestling with a decision.

"You'd better tell me," Shelby said with dread.

Aunt Alicia nodded. "I'm afraid I have some unhappy news for you."

Shelby looked into her aunt's eyes, saw the anguish in her expression, and knew what was coming. She swallowed, determined to be brave. "Jenny's dead, isn't she?"

Aunt Alicia nodded.

"Overdose?"

Her aunt nodded.

"Rick, too?"

Again Aunt Alicia nodded. "The police said the heroin might have been cut with poison. Several other people have died, too."

Tears suddenly filled Shelby's eyes. "Why would somebody do that? How could anyone be so cruel?"

"I don't know," Aunt Alicia admitted.

And then a terrible thought crossed Shelby's mind. Were Jenny and Rick already dead when she'd crept into the bedroom early that morning? If she'd known about the bad smack could she have called the paramedics? Had she *let* her mother die?

Shelby's throat tightened with guilt until she thought she might choke. "I wasn't there for her."

"Honey, you were always there for Jenny. The sad thing is, these last few years, she wasn't there for you."

A tear cascaded down Shelby's cheek, and she wiped it away. "When …?" Shelby hiccupped. "When did this happen?"

"The police think sometime late last night?"

"Did you see them? Did you see Jenny?"

"Yes," Aunt Alicia said and swallowed. It seemed like she might be about to cry, too. "They asked me to identify her."

"What will happen to her now?"

"She was taken to the morgue. We don't have to figure out everything today," Aunt Alicia said gently.

"What about Rick?"

"It's up to his family to…to claim his body."

"And Dog?"

"The police said he'd probably be euthanized."

Shelby looked up sharply. She'd never liked Dog, but it wasn't his fault he'd been mistreated.

"Before I left to come here, I called a pit bull rescue. They were supposed to come and take him away. They'll try to rehabilitate him and find him a good home."

"That would be nice. He never had a good home with Rick," Shelby said sourly. She took in another shuddering breath. "What happens next?"

"You come home with me and stay—for as long as you want."

Sure, because there was nobody else who would take her in.

Shelby looked into her Aunt's eyes once again and saw something she'd seen many times before, but hadn't allowed herself to believe: love.

Shelby's lower lip trembled. "I … I think I need a hug."

"Darlin' they're always free, and I've got a lifetime supply," Aunt Alicia said, and drew Shelby into a gentle embrace.

That's when the tears really began. A torrent of tears. A lifetime's worth of tears. Alicia patted her back, gently rocking her until the sobs quieted.

"You know," Shelby began when she could finally speak again, "even though I never had a happy day with Jenny, I still loved her. Does that make me stupid?"

Aunt Alicia held her tighter. "Not at all. Love is the most powerful emotion of all. And nobody can really explain how and why we love the people we love...even when they may not deserve it. I'm so sorry you never had the opportunity to know Jenny before she got hooked on drugs. She was a wonderful, sweet person. She really loved you and your dad. But it was only weeks after he died that she got hurt."

"The car accident," Shelby said. She'd heard the story—or at least parts of it—most of her life. "She got hooked on pain meds and when they cut her off, she started heroin."

Aunt Alicia nodded. "It happens a lot. It happens far too often. But—despite all the terrible things you've had to go through—I can tell you that no matter what, Jenny always loved you. Sometimes that love blinded her when it came to deciding what was best for you, but she *did* love you. And that you should never doubt."

More tears leaked from Shelby's eyes. "I guess her dying means she'll never suffer again."

"That's right," Aunt Alicia said, pulling Shelby closer once more. "Her suffering is at long last over."

"What will we do now?" Shelby asked with trepidation.

"You're coming home with me. And then we'll figure out a new life for both of us."

Shelby nodded sadly. If nothing else, that would be the best Christmas present she'd ever received.

A CHRISTMAS EVE TO REMEMBER

The conversation in the living room had gone quiet. Blythe stood in the kitchen and looked through the dining room to the living room to see that aunt and niece still sat on the big brown leather sofa, gazing into the fire, and listening to the carols that played on the stereo. It seemed that her guests had run out of things to talk about. Shelby needed to heal; her aunt needed to reconcile herself to a new role in her niece's life. It wouldn't be easy for either of them, and yet Blythe felt that the new bond that the girl and woman had formed during the previous hour would be everlasting.

As quietly as she could, Blythe assembled the various toppings she thought her guests might enjoy, chopping a pepper, an onion, and some mushrooms, then popped the pizza stone into one of the Aga's ovens to warm. When everything was assembled on the kitchen counter, she braved a look into the living room once more and found her guests standing in front of the Christmas tree, examining the ornaments.

Quietly, Blythe traversed the dining room to the living room. "Is everything all right?" she asked.

Alicia looked up. "I think so. What do you think, Shelby?"

Shelby's eyes were bloodshot from crying, and her cheeks were pale, but she nodded nonetheless.

"Are you ladies feeling hungry?" Blythe asked.

Alicia glanced down at her ward.

"This afternoon, Blythe and I made dough for homemade pizza," Shelby said. "Did you know that because of yeast, dough is kind of like a living thing?"

Alicia smiled. "Yes. I think I did hear that at some point." She looked back down at the tree and frowned. "What the...?" She squinted in the dim light. "I swear there's an ornament here with my name on it." She looked back at Blythe, a puzzled expression on her face.

"Really?" Blythe asked.

"When I got here, I found one with my name on it, too," Shelby said and pivoted to show her aunt where that ornament was situated nearby.

"Did you--?" Alicia asked, glancing in Blythe's direction.

Blythe merely shrugged. "Would you ladies like to help make the pizza? I think I've covered just about all the bases when it comes to toppings. The only thing I'm missing are anchovies."

"Yuck!" Shelby squawked.

"Then I take it you're good to go?" Blythe asked.

"I'm sure hungry," Alicia said.

"Me, too," Shelby admitted.

Alicia put her arm around her niece and they started for the kitchen. Blythe let them pass. She'd set the dough on a wooden paddle so that Alicia and Shelby could assemble whatever kind of pizza they desired. She'd leave them to it until it came time to put the pie in the oven. She gravitated toward the beautifully decorated Christmas tree. She gazed at the branches with the ornaments Alicia and Shelby had mentioned just a minute or so before and smiled.

Once again, Blythe Cove Manor had worked its magic. More often than not, life was complicated. But sometimes—and especially at Blythe Cove Manor—miracles did happen.

Blythe's Cocoa
Ingredients
¼ cup unsweetened cocoa powder
½ cup granulated sugar
⅓ cup hot water
4 cups milk
1 teaspoon vanilla extract

Combine the cocoa, sugar, and water in a medium saucepan. Over medium heat, stir constantly until the mixture boils. Cook, stirring constantly for 1 minute.

Stir in the milk and heat, but do not boil. Remove from the heat and add the vanilla; stir well. Serve immediately.

Yield: 4 servings

Clam Chowder
4 cups of shelled clams (about 6 pounds in the shell) or canned or thawed frozen chopped clams, saving the juice
2 cups dry white wine or water

3 ounces bacon (or salt pork), cubed
2 cups diced onion
1 cup diced celery
3 cups diced potatoes
3 sprigs fresh thyme, leaves removed and chopped, or 1 teaspoon dried thyme
1 teaspoon ground black pepper
1 bay leaf
½ cup butter
½ cup all-purpose flour
1½ quarts light cream

In a medium sauce pan, combine the clams and white wine. Heat over a low heat to steam the clams open. Shuck the clams saving the juice. Strain the clam juice and reserve. Rinse the clams clean and roughly chop.

In a large pot, sauté the bacon until brown. Add the onions, celery, thyme, garlic, bay leaf, pepper and sauté for about 5 minutes. Pour the reserved clam juice and the potatoes into the pot. Add enough water to completely cover the potatoes. Stir. Simmer this mixture until the potatoes are tender—about 10 minutes.

Melt the butter in a separate small saucepan. When it is bubbling, add the flour and cook for about 5 minutes stirring often. Set aside. When the potatoes are tender, add the chopped clams and simmer for 2 minutes. Stir the butter and flour mixture into the large pot and continue simmering for another 5 minutes, stirring frequently. This is the chowder base.

In a separate saucepan, scald the cream by heating it until small bubbles form around the edges of the pan. Do not boil. Stir the hot scalded cream into the large pot, mix together and remove from the heat. Serve immediately.

YIELD: 6 to 8 servings

Easy Peanut Butter Fudge

Ingredients

2 sticks butter (one cup), plus more for greasing the pan

1 cup smooth peanut butter

1 teaspoon vanilla extract

1 pound confectioners' sugar

½ cup peanuts (optional)

Combine the butter and peanut butter in a microwavable bowl. Cover with a paper towel and microwave for 2 minutes on high. Stir and microwave on high for 2 more minutes. Add the vanilla and confectioners' sugar to the peanut butter mixture and stir to combine. The mixture will become firm. Spread into an 8 by 8-inch pan lined with buttered aluminum foil or parchment paper. Cover and refrigerate for at least 2 hours. Cut into 1-inch squares.

Yield: 64 squares

IF YOU ENJOYED ...

If you enjoyed *An Unexpected Visitor*, please consider reviewing it on your favorite online review site. Thank you!

Find our more about Lorraine and her work on her website
www.LorraineBartlett.com

GRAPE EXPECTATIONS

A TALE FROM BLYTHE COVE MANOR

DISCRIPTION

GRAPE EXPECTATIONS

Young heiress Dolly Madison arrives on Martha's Vineyard with an agenda to discover and taste the great wines of this picturesque island off the coast of Massachusetts ... only to learn there are none. What she will find, however, is far more compelling—and could just change her life.

Blythe Calvert looked up from the counter where she was assembling ingredients to bake a batch of cookies in Blythe Cove Manor's well-appointed kitchen when the sound of tires on gravel captured her attention. Time to greet her newest guest.

Blythe stepped behind the small reception desk. Through the glass of the double doors of her bed and breakfast's entrance, she could see Ed Thomas's taxi pull up in front. He got out and walked to the back, where he retrieved a suitcase and a large canvas tote from the back of the van. His passenger, a young woman clad in a blue-and-white floral sundress that was perhaps a size too small, a large floppy straw hat, and sunglasses, stepped out of the back seat and strode toward the inn without a backward glance, leaving the door open and Ed to trail behind her with the luggage. It wasn't part of the services he offered when delivering people from the Oaks Bluff ferry to Blythe Cove Manor.

The woman entered the inn, letting the door swing shut behind her—right in Ed's face.

Oh dear, was she going to be one of *those* kinds of guests?

"Good morning," Blythe called cheerfully. "You must be Dolly Madison. That's a very interesting name." She pushed the registration book and a pen toward the woman.

Dolly's expression hardened. Obviously, Blythe was not the first to mention her moniker.

"My mother thought it was hilarious. But I've been teased about it my whole life. 'Gonna throw a party, Dolly? Know anybody at the White House, Dolly?'" Her lips flattened into a tense line. "Yeah, I've heard it all. And then she didn't even spell it the same as the original Dolley Madison."

Blythe smiled and tried again. "What brings you to the island?"

Dolly looked around, as though to make sure no one was nearby to eavesdrop. "I'm running away from home," she whispered quite seriously.

Blythe merely blinked at that statement.

Again, Dolly looked around her. "I inherited a million bucks from a great aunt I didn't even know existed and everybody I know wants a piece of the action." She brushed an imaginary piece of lint from her shoulder strap, flaunting the diamond tennis bracelet on her left wrist.

Blythe blinked again.

Ed strolled up to the reception desk, plopping the long-handled canvas bag at Dolly's feet, then gave her the bad news about the fare. She opened her purse, peeled off the exact amount, and handed it to him.

"Thank you for bringing in Ms. Madison's luggage," Blythe said. "It was kind of you to accommodate her."

Dolly took no hint that a tip was warranted.

"I'd like to go to my room, please," Dolly said, sounding bored.

Blythe handed over the old-fashioned skeleton key. "It's the Cove Room, on the second floor to the left as you top the landing."

Dolly scrutinized the key. "Don't you have electronic locks for security?"

"They'd be pretty useless if the power goes off."

"Does that happen a lot?"

"No, and we do have a generator, but you never know."

Dolly frowned, then looked around. "Where's the bellboy?"

"We don't have one. Guests are responsible for their own luggage," Blythe explained.

Dolly's frown deepened. "If I'd known that, I'd have demanded a ground-floor room."

"I'm sorry, but they're all taken."

"What about the cottages?"

"Fully booked, I'm afraid. As I mentioned when we spoke on the phone, we had a cancelation, which is why your room was available."

Dolly looked from her luggage to Ed.

He smiled. "Have a nice stay."

Blythe and Ed watched as Dolly picked up the tote and tossed it over her shoulder, then picked up her suitcase and marched toward the stairs. Neither spoke until Dolly disappeared from sight.

"I'm sorry about the tip. It sounds like she could well afford to give one."

Ed merely shook his head. "Don't bother calling me back when it comes time for the young lady to leave. I won't be available," he said and turned on his heel.

Blythe frowned. "I'm sorry, Ed."

He turned back to face her. "Ms. Madison and I had a very interesting conversation during the ride from the ferry."

"And?" Blythe asked.

Ed smirked. "She has some pretty wonky ideas about the island. I didn't want to spoil her illusions. Have a great day, Blythe," he called and sashayed out the door.

What had he meant by that cryptic statement?

Blythe soon found out some ten minutes later when Dolly reappeared in the large living room.

"Hello! Anybody here?"

Blythe set down the spatula she'd been using to mix raisins and walnuts into her oatmeal cookie dough, wiped her hands on a dish towel, and called, "Coming!"

She found Dolly standing in the center of the room, looking impatient.

"How can I help you?" Blythe asked.

"I was wondering if there's a company on the island that has tours of all the wineries. I wanted to come for the harvest, but I was told the island practically shuts down after Labor Day. But while I'm here, I'm anxious to taste every brand of wine you guys have got."

Anxious or eager? Brand or vintage?

And was this the topic Ed had decided to let Blythe tackle?

"I'm not sure I understand," Blythe hedged.

"I want to see all the vineyards on the island. I want to go to tastings and buy some of the great wines."

Blythe chose her words carefully. "I'm assuming you aren't aware of the history of the island?"

"What's to know? It was named after somebody named Martha and she made wine."

"Folklore has it that the island was named by British explorer Bartholomew Gosnold after his infant daughter, Martha," she conceded, "but the grapevines were wild."

"Wild, tame—what's the difference?"

"Wild grapes are aren't suitable for winemaking," Blythe explained.

"Then why did some jackass name the place a vineyard?"

Blythe forced a smile and shrugged. "Just one of those things."

Dolly glowered. "What am I supposed to do trapped on this island for a week with nothing to do and nowhere to go?"

"There're plenty of places to see—and lots of things to do,"

Blythe assured her. "And if you just want to relax, this is the perfect place." She gestured toward the patio and the gardens beyond.

Dolly's expression remained unhappy. "I'd be bored out of my mind."

Blythe reached behind the reception desk and pulled out a loose-leaf notebook. "You can flip through the pages and look at brochures for the restaurants and other attractions on the island."

"Attractions? You mean like water parks?"

"Uh, no. We don't have a water park. But we do have a Summer Film Festival."

"Art films are boring."

"The annual August fireworks display happens during your stay."

"I'd get a stiff neck looking up at the sky for a long time."

"We've got wonderful beaches," Blythe tried again, "and if you don't want to swim, you can borrow one of our stand-up paddle boards."

"There are sharks in the ocean. They could bite me—even *kill* me."

Blythe sighed. "Well, I'm sure you'll find something to do when you look at all the tourist information in the book. If you'll excuse me, I have some cookies to bake."

"Cookies?" Dolly asked, sounding more interested in that than Blythe's other suggestions.

"Yes. I keep a cookie jar filled with them so guests can snack on them during the day and evening."

"Can I help?"

Blythe blinked, startled by the request. "Uh, I don't usually allow guests in the kitchen."

"Maybe you should offer cooking classes to your guests."

"I've considered it," Blythe admitted.

"If you won't let me help, can I at least watch?"

"I suppose so." Blythe turned and headed for the kitchen with Dolly practically at her heels.

The AGA cooker was up to speed, all Blythe had to do was drop the dough onto the prepared baking sheets and tuck them into the oven.

"Oatmeal raisin with walnuts?" Dolly asked.

"Uh-huh." Blythe set the timer.

"I love them," Dolly said, sounding less like the petulant kid she had been not five minutes before and more like a delighted child who wanted to please. She leaned against the counter, watching Blythe's every move.

"Do you know how to bake?"

Dolly nodded. "I'm not very good at it, but I think I could be. After I got my inheritance, I immediately changed my phone number, quit my job, bought myself a new wardrobe, and have been in hiding. I live in a luxury condo, but I've got my eye on a house in a swanky neighborhood with a gourmet kitchen. I'm waiting for a call from a real estate agent."

"Sounds like you've got everything figured out."

"I still don't know what I want to do with my life, but I figured I should try to come up with a plan. That's why I came to the island. I thought I could learn about wine and become one of those snobs that advise other people on what wines to drink and buy."

"You mean a sommelier?"

"I guess."

Blythe thought about it. "Perhaps I could help you in that area. I have a friend who runs a farm on the north end of the island. He actually does have grapevines and bottles wine for himself."

"But it's not a *real* vineyard?" Dolly asked.

"No. He supplies a number of local restaurants with fresh produce during the summer."

"And what's he do in the winter?"

"He teaches third grade at the Oak Bluffs Elementary school."

"What's his name?" Dolly asked.

"Josh Frederick. I think you'd like him."

"When can I meet him?"

"Maybe as soon as tomorrow. When the cookies come out of the oven, I'll give him a call."

"How will I get to his farm?"

"Sorry?" Blythe asked.

"I heard that taxi driver say he wouldn't drive me anymore. What am I supposed to do to get around the island?"

Be nicer to people, Blythe wanted to say but bit her tongue. "I'm sure we can find a way. Let me think about it."

"Okay," Dolly said quietly. "I'm not a bad person," she defended herself, "but since I inherited all that money, people try to take advantage of me. I'm not going to let that happen," she said fiercely.

Blythe nodded. Despite her arrogance, she suspected that there might be a vulnerable person hiding behind Dolly's bravado. Maybe Josh Frederick was just the person to persuade Dolly that kind and generous people abounded—if one only knew where to look.

CHAPTER 2

*D*olly awoke early the next morning with the sun cascading through the window of her pretty room. She'd left the blinds up the night before because she'd been fascinated by the number of stars she could see far from the glare of city lights.

The Sandpiper Restaurant had been within walking distance of Blythe Cove Manor, and she'd turned down the invitation of four of the other guests to join them for dinner the evening before. Had they heard about her windfall? Had they made the invitation just so that she would pick up the check? She wasn't about to fall for that old ruse, but she had to admit that eating by herself at a table overlooking the ocean was rather lonely. She ate her very first lobster—what locals called "bugs"—and then she'd walked back to the inn, frequently looking over her shoulder in case there was a mugger nearby looking for prey.

She got up, showered, and dressed in Capri pants, a sleeveless blouse, and sandals, and came down to Blythe Cove Manor's dining room, which was devoid of other guests. It was then she remembered that breakfast wasn't served until seven o'clock. She still had at least an hour to go until then. She peeked into the kitchen and found Blythe at work, chopping vegetables for the custom-made omelets guests could order. But she also inhaled the scent of cinnamon from something baking in that amazing AGA cooker. She'd never seen such a stove and had listened enraptured the afternoon before when Blythe had explained how it worked.

Blythe had her back to the dining room as Dolly tiptoed closer to the kitchen. She cleared her throat and Blythe whirled.

"Oh, my! You startled me."

"Sorry. Even though the dining room isn't yet open, I was hoping I might be able to get a cup of coffee."

"I usually wait until six-thirty to make it but I guess I can start a little early today," Blythe said.

The back door opened and an older, rather matronly woman entered. "Morning, Blythe."

"Hi, Carol. Ready to start the day? I was just telling Ms. Madison here that I would get the coffee going."

"I can get it," Carol said and started for the dining room. "Hello."

"Hi," Dolly said and watched the woman for a moment before she turned back to Blythe, who had resumed her chopping. "Um, were you able to find me a ride to that farm you were telling me about?"

Knife in hand, Blythe looked over her shoulder. "Carol has to pass it on her way home. Perhaps she'd be willing to give you a lift."

"Good."

Blythe turned. "Uh, Dolly, if she's willing, I hope you'll remember to thank her."

Dolly rolled her eyes. "I'm not a jerk."

Blythe raised an eyebrow before returning to her work.

Carol returned and filled the carafe with water before heading back to the dining room. Dolly followed her because there was nothing else to do. Coming to this bed and breakfast might have been a mistake. Perhaps she should have gone to a big city—like San Francisco—and then she could have disappeared and nobody would know who she was or how much money she had.

And yet, as she thought about it, Blythe Cove Manor's proprietress wouldn't have had a clue she was worth big bucks if she hadn't opened her big mouth and mentioned it. She could have just been Little Miss Anonymous. And what would she do in a big city, anyway, except be as lonely as she felt right then?

Dolly sat at one of the tables and looked through the French doors out to the garden and then the cove beyond. It sure was pretty here, but it didn't look like there was much to do—at least for someone traveling alone. And she wondered what time Carol worked until so that Dolly could go to the farm and talk to Josh Frederick about wine. Maybe he'd be willing to talk about other stuff, too.

She sighed. It would be a long morning.

CHAPTER 3

It was after ten when Carol—Dolly never did learn her last name—was ready to head for home. Her vehicle was a beat-up, faded red Chevy truck that bounced along the uneven asphalt as she steered north toward Oak Bluffs.

"How long are you staying on the island?"

Dolly wasn't sure she should answer truthfully. Could this woman know about her millions? Could she be trying to worm her way into Dolly's confidences?

"A while," she answered vaguely. The truth was, she was booked at Blythe Cove Manor for six more days, although it sounded like the week might be a bust. She'd have to consider her options. Ms. Calvert might want to charge her for an early cancelation if she decided to curtail her stay. She might now be rich, but she wouldn't forget how it felt to be poor.

"Do you know the guy that owns Frederick Farm?"

Carol's gaze remained on the road. "Josh? Sure. Ever since he was a little squirt."

"What's he like?"

"Oh, a great guy. Kind, good-looking," she said and waggled her eyebrows suggestively.

"Ms. Calvert said he was a teacher and a farmer."

"Yes. The farm has been in his family for four generations. His parents retired a few years back and he's taken it over."

"Sounds like a big job for just one man."

"He has help," Carol said and braked.

Up ahead, Dolly could see a dirt road off to their left and as they pulled onto it, she saw a faded painted sign that said FREDERICK FARM. Underneath were painted the hours: 10 am to 4 pm. She glanced at the truck's dashboard clock and saw that it was nearly ten thirty. The place should be hopping. But instead, as they approached a barn and what looked to be a produce stand, there was nobody around the place.

Carol stopped the truck and shifted into park. "Here you go."

"How will I get back to Blythe Cove Manor? Will you pick me up and take me there?"

"Sorry, honey, but I've got plans later this afternoon. Don't worry. Blythe will make sure you get back to the Manor."

Dolly opened the cab's door, grabbed her purse and got out, slamming the door. Then she remembered what Blythe had told her. "Thanks for the ride."

"You're welcome. See you tomorrow at the Manor."

And with that, Carol reversed the truck and then drove back the way she came. Dolly watched until she reached the main road and continued north. Now what was she supposed to do?

She heard the sound of what she figured were chickens squawking in the barn and headed in that direction. Maybe there was someone there who could tell her where to find Josh Frederick.

"Hello?" Dolly called as she approached the open barn door. She stepped onto the concrete floor inside, where scattered corn was being pecked by a number of chickens and wondered if they'd bite her bare toes. A door at the back of the barn was also open, with bright sunlight shining through. "Hello!" she called again.

"Can I help you?" came a man's voice from the back as a silhouette appeared in the far doorway.

"My name is Dolly. Blythe Calvert sent me to see you. That is if you're Josh Frederick."

The man approached. As Carol had said, he was good-looking, but his expression wasn't all that welcoming. Maybe he wasn't as nice as Carol had indicated.

"Yes, she called. Said you wanted to taste my wine."

"Do you have a vineyard?"

He shook his head, then jerked a thumb over his shoulder. "I've got ten vines. It's enough to make a couple of cases every fall."

"Do you sell them?"

He shook his head. "But I do serve them when we have a Taste of the Farm celebration."

"And when's your next one?"

"This weekend, as a matter of fact. It's sold out."

Dolly frowned, disappointed. "Oh."

"But I could use some help at the event. One of the waitresses canceled on me."

Dolly blinked. "You want to hire me to wait on tables?"

"Why not? That is if you're willing to tie on an apron—and a smile." That last sounded like a dig. Who did this guy think he was?

Dolly–a waitress?

"It's the only way you'll get to taste my wine," he teased.

Dolly thought it over. Why not help out at the little shindig? She had nothing better to do during her stay on the island.

"Okay. You've got a deal. When do I start?"

"Right now."

It turned out the farm wasn't deserted after all—everybody had just parked their vehicles behind the barn. Dolly was introduced to a number of men and women decked out in jeans, T-shirts, and work boots, which made her feel a little silly for dressing so casually. But nobody mentioned her rather inappropriate attire.

Dolly never worked so hard in her life. It turned out that Josh Frederick possessed unquestionable Simon Legree tendencies. Toting barges and lifting bales would have been easier. As it was, Dolly was asked to help lift and arrange bales of hay, as that was part of the décor for the upcoming farm-to-table dinner party. Still, she had to admit that Josh worked just as hard as those in his employ. And there was plenty of water and snacks, and the scheduled breaks were scattered throughout the day.

With the grass cut and the gardens weeded, the outside decorating was complete, it was understood that tomorrow most of the women would be helping with the food prep, while the guys set up the tables and chairs for the ticketed guests. It would take a lot of chopping and grilling to feed fifty hungry people. An older man, by the name of Benny Metzger, was in charge of the barbeque, and he'd been smoking the beef for a day so that it would be ready on Saturday.

A palpable air of anticipation seemed to hover over the little organic farm, and Dolly wasn't immune to it, either.

By the time Josh drove her back to Blythe Cove Manor later that evening, Dolly found it difficult to stifle a yawn, and it was all she could do to keep her eyes open.

"My friend Lucy will pick you up tomorrow before eight. Can you be ready?"

"Of course." At least Dolly wouldn't have to wait for Carol to give her a lift to the farm, and she felt lucky someone was willing to give her a ride for the next day's tasks. Dolly had to admit, she was looking forward to seeing how the whole farm-to-table dinner would play out, although she wasn't sure why.

"See you tomorrow," Josh said noncommittedly when Dolly closed the cab's passenger side door. She stood by the inn's front entrance and watched as he took off down the drive and then until he was out of sight, not sure what to make of the man.

Interesting could cover a lot of territory.

Too tired to walk to the restaurant, Dolly meandered into Blythe Cove's dining room, once again finding the cookie jar full to the brim. *Blythe must bake all day,* she marveled and took a handful of the chocolate chip cookies. The water in the carafe was piping hot, and she made herself a cup of tea before she sat down at one of the empty tables and enjoyed her repast.

Most everyone else must have gone to dinner, she figured, although if she craned her neck to the right she could see a couple sharing glasses of wine in the Adirondack chairs on the patio that overlooked the sea.

How lucky they are, Dolly lamented. *I'll bet they have no issues when it comes to who does what and who pays for what in their relationship.*

While she wasn't unhappy that her future was secure and if she lived prudently she would have no financial problems for the rest of her life, living in fear of being taken advantage of was exhausting. Mistrusting everyone she met seemed downright wrong. But once word of her inheritance had come through, people she'd barely known in school, at former jobs, and even strangers had appeared to beg for and berate her for money. It tended to sour one on mankind at large.

But she had to admit that, though she was almost at the brink of exhaustion while working at the farm, she had enjoyed it and the camaraderie she had felt with the others who shared the workload.

Her accountant had wanted to invest every nickel of her inheritance into personal IRAs, stocks, and bonds, but she didn't really know the man. Was he honest? She'd heard of people being taken for everything they owned by people professing to be business managers. Superstars like Johnny Depp and Rihanna had been swindled out of millions because they trusted others with their fortunes, only to find themselves broke and at the mercy of the IRS, which had no patience for excuses.

And Dolly had been impressed with the entire Frederick Farm operation. Josh seemed to know what he was doing. He *seemed* kind. He *listened* to the people working for him. And according to Blythe, he *was* successful. All that, and he still needed a day job teaching.

But most importantly, he made wine. Wine Dolly was eager to try.

He'd said that part of the bargain to work for him would be that she'd get to try his version of the nectar of the Gods, and she was bound and determined to hold him to it.

Only crumbs littered the white paper napkin before her, and the pretty bone china mug with a vibrant pink hollyhock motif had been thoroughly drained. And though it was still light, Dolly firmly believed that she would sleep through the night ... and dream about Frederick Farm's wine.

ONCE AGAIN, Dolly awoke early, but instead of dreading the day, she was filled with anticipation and had to keep from singing out loud while taking her shower.

And again, when she entered the dining room early that morning, she found it empty, but the coffee pot was full—and freshly made. She poured herself a cup and wandered toward the kitchen where Blythe once more stood in front of her AGA cooker. "What's on the menu this morning?"

Blythe turned. "Blueberry muffins. They'll be ready in about ten minutes. Can you wait that long?"

Dolly's smile was organic. "Yes."

"Good. The west side of my property is full of wild blueberries. I picked them this morning when they were still dew-covered."

"Sounds like the perfect photo op."

Blythe laughed—a golden sound. "As a matter of fact, I *did* take a photo. It turned out well, too. I might upload it to my website."

"You update your own website?"

"Some programs make it easy. You might almost say…magical."

There was something about the way Blythe said that word, *magical,* that sent a shiver up Dolly's spine.

"So, how did you enjoy your day at Frederick Farm?"

"I got hired to help with the Taste of the Farm Celebration."

"Really?" Blythe asked, although she didn't sound at all surprised.

"Tonight we're serving dinner to fifty people. I have a hard time imaging how Josh is going to pull that off."

"No doubt with aplomb," Blythe said and laughed. Somehow, it sounded almost musical. "Once again, you're up early."

"Someone working at the event is supposed to pick me up before eight this morning."

"Then you'd better have a hearty breakfast before you leave. I have a feeling it's going to be a challenging day for you."

In what way? Dolly was tempted to ask, but then she didn't. Perhaps she really didn't want the surprise to be spoiled.

"I'd be happy to make you whatever you want for breakfast," Blythe said.

Dolly thought about it. "My mother used to make me a poached egg on toast. I haven't had one for such a long time."

"With toast soldiers?" Blythe asked.

"Yes, please," Dolly said and smiled, remembering her long-dead parent and happier days from her childhood.

And as breakfasts go, it was one filled with nostalgia. Almost as if her mom had ordained it.

And just as Dolly took her last bite of toast, she heard a horn outside go *beep-beep.*

"My ride is here," Dolly said and made a grab for her duffle, which held the white blouse and dark slacks she would need to wear that evening when she would play waitress to the farm's dinner guests.

"Have a wonderful time. And remember everything," Blythe wished.

Remember everything? Dolly thought as she rushed out the door to climb into the truck that awaited to take her to her second day of gainful employment since she'd become an heiress.

For some reason, she felt sure there might be some kind of magic involved with the day, too.

CHAPTER 5

"*Y*ou're not from around here," Lucy St. James said as they bounced along Blythe Cove Manor's gravel drive that led to the main road.

Although Dolly had met her erstwhile chauffeur the day before, they hadn't had any time to converse. "No. I'm … just visiting." She wasn't about to say she was on vacation—hiding out —and why. The wind from the truck's open windows whipped the graying sandy hair that had escaped from Lucy's ponytail and also spoiled the careful comb job Dolly had given herself. Lucy must have been at least fifteen or twenty years older than Dolly but exuded a confidence that eluded the younger woman.

"Is this your first farm weekend?" Dolly asked.

"Heck no. More like tenth or twelfth. This is Josh's third year doing them. He usually hosts three dinners every summer and one in the fall—those are for the locals and are a lot more fun because I get to spend time with my friends. That said, don't give him any ideas about throwing a winter bash," she said and grinned. The laugh lines around her eyes were deeply etched. She must smile a lot, Dolly decided.

"What kind of food will we be cooking today?"

"Some of us will be baking the desserts—the blueberries are ripe, so my guess is there'd be cobbler and crisp on the menu. That's what we had last year."

"I've never had either."

"Then you've got a wonderful surprise awaiting you. Of course, first, we have to pick them."

"Out in a field?" Dolly asked, not certain she wanted to know the answer.

"That's where they grow."

Dolly had worn jeans and flats, but she wasn't sure they'd be appropriate for fieldwork. Lucy wore cutoffs, but she also wore white socks and heavy duty boots. Maybe she had other clothes and shoes in the back of the truck. Dolly crossed her fingers and hoped Josh might pick her for some other work.

It didn't take long before they pulled up in front of Frederick Farm, which was already bustling with activity. Lucy parked the truck around the back side of the barn, and they grabbed their bags before heading to the big farmhouse. Lucy showed Dolly where to stow her things before they reported to Josh, who was holding court in the home's dining room. He sat at the head of the big oak table with a clipboard in front of him, calling off names and jobs. And, just like she feared, Dolly was included in the berry picking detail. At least she and Lucy would be working together.

In all, six had been assigned to pick berries; four women and two men. They stopped at the barn to grab straw hats big enough to protect their heads and necks, and each person was given a plastic container that was clipped around their middles, kind of like a fanny pack. "That's what we'll put the blueberries in," Lucy said. And then headed to the blueberry patch.

"I don't know how to pick blueberries," Dolly admitted as she buckled on the container, feeling like a walking bushel basket.

"It's easy. I'll show you, and you'll be an expert within five minutes."

The others were obviously well acquainted with the work, and Dolly felt a little self-conscious, but Lucy had been right. She explained to Dolly that she mustn't pull the berries from the bush, but to put her fingers under a cluster of them, then wiggle them around until they fell. Anything that didn't fall, wasn't ready for eating. "And you want the ones that look kind of dusty, too. We don't wash them until right before they're ready to use."

"That's good to know," Dolly said, but she followed Lucy's lead and wiped the dust away and tried one. Sweet and delicious.

They worked steadily, the others talking and joking among themselves as they picked while Dolly concentrated on the task at hand. After almost an hour, one of the other women said they'd picked enough, and they headed back to the barn where they dumped all six containers into a bigger tote and Lucy and Dolly took it back to the house, bypassing the rental company's truck that was delivering tables, chairs, plates, silverware, and glassware.

"Wow—Josh doesn't have everything he needs for his party?"

"Why own it and have to store it when he only needs it four times a year?"

Dolly nodded. "Do they set it all up, too?"

Lucy shook her head. "No. The guys will set out the tables and chairs and Donna and her crew will set the table."

"Josh doesn't grow everything himself, does he?"

Lucy shook her head. "But everything is raised right here on the island, including the meat."

"Like what?"

"Josh has deals with other farmers for mushrooms, flowers—even some that are edible—and lots of other vegetables. It's all farm-to-table fare."

"And what about the wine?" Dolly asked.

"Wine? Oh, mean the stuff Josh bottles?"

Dolly nodded.

Lucy wrinkled her nose. "It's drinkable, but not if you consider yourself a wine snob."

"But it's made here on Martha's Vineyard. Is it the only wine made here?"

Lucy shrugged. "Maybe other islanders have vines. I wouldn't know about that. When I'm not working for Josh in the summers, I'm a math teacher at Martha's Vineyard Regional High School."

Math had never been Dolly's core strength. "Is that how you met him?"

"He teaches elementary students, but essentially yes."

"Is he married?" Dolly asked.

"No, but he's got more on his plate than looking for a wife, if that's what you're getting at."

"I wasn't," Dolly said flatly. "I was just making conversation."

"What do you do?" Lucy asked.

"Um…I'm between jobs at the moment, but I did work in a factory that makes clips that hold car batteries. It was really boring."

"What would you *like* to do?"

Dolly was about to say *learn about wine*, but then thought better of it. Dolly didn't want Lucy to tell the others she'd been suckered in by the island's name. "I'm not sure."

They made it back to the farmhouse with its weathered shingles just as Josh stepped onto the porch. "You're just in time, ladies. We need to get baking." He caught Dolly's gaze. "Do you think you're ready for this?"

"Looking forward to it," Dolly said and realized that she actually was.

CHAPTER 6

*D*olly had never worked as a waitress, but she had once worked in a fast-food restaurant and understood the concept of getting food to the customer while it was still hot. That hadn't been a priority with the salad course, but once the entree went out, it was a mad rush for the four waitresses to serve all twenty-five couples. And then came the dessert course. Because she'd helped make them, Dolly found herself watching in tense anticipation, looking for critical remarks or unhappy expressions, but everyone seemed just as enchanted with the blueberry concoctions as she'd been while helping to make them.

And, of course, she paid close attention to the wine flights. As Lucy had hinted, not many of the patrons seemed all that enthused with the Frederick Farm red, but there were a few who complimented the wine, but then whole-heartedly encouraged their glasses to be filled with a more mainstream selection.

And she'd studied Josh's expression while listening to the criticism, which could have been described as either stoic or unfeeling, something she was pretty sure was not part of his usual countenance. It made her even more desirous of tasting said wine.

The sun was setting as the last of the guests climbed back in their cars and left the farm. It was time to break down the set, rinse the dishes, and pack things away so that the rental firm could pick them up the next day. Josh paid and thanked everyone for their work before the others wandered off to collect their vehicles and go home.

By that time, some thirteen hours after she'd left Blythe Cove Manor, Dolly found herself verging on the brink of exhaustion. The sun had long since sunk into the ocean when at last Josh was ready to again take her back to Blythe Cove Manor, where a soothing shower and then a blessedly comfortable bed awaited her.

But as Josh called to her she remembered his promise.

"You can't take me back yet. You said if I worked for you I'd get to taste your wine."

Josh shrugged. "Are you sure you want to? I mean, you saw the reaction from my guests who tried it."

"So? I can't stand strawberries, but that doesn't mean I can't understand that others could love them."

He blinked at her.

"You know what I mean," she said defensively.

"I guess so."

"So, when do I get to taste it?"

"How about right now?"

Josh set two wine glasses on the dining room table and produced a corkscrew. A wagon wheel light fixture hung low above the table as he took his seat and poured. She'd expected a red and was surprised when a golden stream filled her glass. They clinked glasses and drank.

Dolly wasn't put off by the taste. It was sweeter than she would have thought. The guests must have all been wine snobs.

Josh was watching her. "Well?"

"I like it."

He frowned and shook his head.

"I mean it," Dolly said and took another healthy sip. "I mean, it's not rot gut."

For a long moment, Josh just stared at her, and then he laughed. "I guess that was supposed to be a compliment."

"It was," Dolly said sincerely. "I'm impressed."

"You're the only one," he muttered and took another sip. "But that's the reason for my trip."

"Trip?" Dolly asked.

"I'm going to spend the next three weeks in California. Napa Valley, in fact."

"Doing what?"

"Hopefully learning how to make great wine."

"Would you change jobs—leave the island?" Dolly asked.

Josh shook his head. "I teach to earn a living, but my real job is this farm. I'm the fifth generation to run it, and I don't intend to be the last in my family to own it. But I also want to make more than just a barely drinkable wine."

"So you're essentially going back to school?"

"In essence."

"But who will take care of the chickens, the cow, the goats, and the crops?"

"My parents. They retired to North Carolina, but they have no problem coming back to help out. And since they taught me everything I know about farming, I know Fredrick Farm will be in more than capable hands while I'm gone."

Dolly sighed and wrapped her fingers around the stem of her glass. "I wish I had my future planned out like you do."

"Lucy told me you were between jobs."

Dolly nodded.

"What is it you really want to do, Dolly?"

"It sounds stupid but after being here at the farm for the past two days and working with the others, I think I'd like to cook for people. But I can't."

"Why not?"

"Because."

"Now you sound like a child. Just answer the question from your heart," he encouraged.

"It's because of my name," she groused.

Josh looked confused. "Dolly?"

"Dolly Madison!"

Josh just stared at her. "So what?"

Dolly heaved an exasperated sigh. "I've been teased my entire life about being a hostess, entertaining people, parties, parties, parties!" she almost shouted.

He just kept staring at her.

"So. What?" Josh repeated.

Dolly rose from her chair. "I'm tired of it."

"Then why don't you just change your name?"

Dolly stood there, blinking at him.

"Either that or live up to it."

"What do you mean?"

"Dolley Madison was an important historical figure. She may have had a reputation for giving parties, but she did much more than that. She helped define the role of First Lady of our country. As the wife of our fourth president, she showed by example what it meant to lead during turbulent times."

"Like?"

He frowned. "Did you ever hear of the War of 1812?"

"Sort of," Dolly admitted with a half shrug. "That was history. Who cares about it now?"

Josh leveled a hard gaze at her. "'Those who do not learn from history are bound to repeat it,'" he quoted. "But in this case, you might want to walk in the shadow of Mrs. Madison."

What did that mean?

Josh looked at his watch. "It's getting late and I have to leave on the early ferry. I'd better drive you back to the Manor."

"Thank you."

Josh got up and pulled the keys from his jeans pocket, but

Dolly insisted on rinsing the glasses and placing them in the dishwasher before they left the house.

They didn't speak during the drive to Blythe Cove Manor. Dolly had way too much to think about.

And think she did.

It wasn't often that Blythe waited up until all her guests had safely returned from their travels on the island, but for some reason, she felt she needed to do so that evening. With her tabby cat, Martha, by her side, she'd stationed herself on the big leather couch in the Manor's living room/lobby, with a glass of sherry and her current book club's selection.

It was after ten when she heard the sound of tires on the gravel drive, muffled voices, and then the slam of a car door. Seconds later, the front door opened, and Blythe turned to see Dolly enter. She paused, waved, and then Blythe heard the sound of the vehicle's engine as it pulled away. Dolly kept watch until the vehicle's hum faded before she closed the door and seemed startled to find Blythe's gaze upon her.

"I'm sorry. I didn't mean to disturb you."

"I was just having a glass of sherry. Would you like to join me?"

Dolly's smile was tentative. "Yes, thanks."

Blythe nodded toward the big coffee table before her where a crystal carafe and another glass sat on a polished silver tray. "Help yourself."

Dolly took the adjacent chair, poured the sherry and paused, looking unsure of herself. "Are we supposed to toast?"

"We don't have to, but it might be nice," Blythe said. She picked up her own glass. "To finding just what we need."

Dolly looked a little confused, but then she tipped her glass in salute and took a minute sip. "Wow. That's pretty powerful stuff."

Blythe smiled and sipped her sherry. "How did the dinner go?"

"Really well. It was…a surprising day."

"In what way?"

"I learned so much—about farming, about the island, cooking, and making people happy with something as simple as blueberry crisp."

"I get the feeling you haven't been much acquainted with the concept of happiness."

Dolly's gaze dipped and she nodded. "Since I inherited all that cash, I found out the hard way that money can't buy happiness or solve all your problems."

"What's your biggest problem?"

Dolly hesitated. "I don't have a purpose in life. I don't think I ever did, but it didn't really hit me until an hour or so ago when Josh asked me what I really wanted in life."

"And then it occurred to you?"

Dolly nodded. "Yeah, but it sounds really stupid."

"Nonsense," Blythe assured her, nodding for Dolly to continue.

"I want to make myself happy by making other people happy … with food."

Blythe took a slow sip of her sherry. "I don't think that's stupid at all. Part of what I do here at Blythe Cove Manor is to start my guests' day off with food. They say breakfast is the most important meal of the day. It shouldn't only be nutritious, but it should soothe the soul."

Dolly looked around the big living room, taking in all the

comforts of a welcoming home. "There's definitely something about Blythe Cove Manor that soothes *my* soul. But I've felt conflicted, too. And I don't know what I need to do to make that feeling go away."

"Well, defining your goals might help. Do you aspire to be a chef?"

Dolly wrinkled her nose. "I don't think so. I mean, I never really prepared meals. I was thinking more about doing what you do. Your breakfasts are amazing. Would you teach me to bake like you do?"

Blythe looked at the young woman, feeling an amalgam of pity and compassion. "I don't think I'm the right person for that. I just bake cookies and muffins." And very well, too, but Blythe suspected Dolly wanted much more than to be told how to measure and mix ingredients. She thought about the request for a few long moments.

Dolly looked crestfallen.

"However," Blythe began, "I happen to know that the Epicurean Bakery in Vineyard Haven is looking for help—and they'll provide training. It could be a wonderful learning experience."

Dolly looked thoughtful. "Maybe."

"It's hard work, but I think the rewards would be more than worthwhile."

"That would mean I'd have to stay on the island for a while."

"Did you have any other plans?"

Dolly shook her head and looked thoughtful as she took another sip of sherry. "Could you put in a good word for me?"

"I'll give the owner, Marcie Jenkins, a call tomorrow morning. She's eager to fill the position. I'm willing to bet she'll give you an interview immediately. Maybe you could even start tomorrow."

Dolly's eyes lit up. "You think?"

Blythe smiled and nodded.

"But if I get the job, where will I stay? It's high summer. You said you're booked solid for the rest of the season."

"I am. But I do have a room that I seldom rent out. It's tiny. A bed, a dresser, and a minuscule bathroom with just a stall shower."

"I could handle that," Dolly assured her.

"Let's see how tomorrow goes and then we'll talk about the rest of it, okay?"

"Okay."

Blythe finished the last of her drink, set the glass on the tray and stood. "It's been a long day. Tomorrow comes mighty early here at the Manor."

Dolly downed the last of her drink and set her glass on the tray, too. Blythe picked it up and looked down at her cat. "Time for bed, Martha."

The cat got up, stretched its legs, and jumped down from the couch. "We'll talk more in the morning."

"I'd like that," Dolly said, sounding encouraged.

Blythe gave her a smile and headed toward the kitchen. She had a feeling something good was in the offing.

CHAPTER 8

*D*olly got the job.

If she thought that working at the Taste of the Farm Celebration was hard, then Dolly had no concept of hard work. At first, her new boss, Marcie Jenkins, had given Dolly the bottom-of-the-barrel jobs. Washing pots, stacking trays, and chopping fruits for pies, muffins, cobblers, and crisps, but within a week, Marcie began teaching her the ins and outs of making artisanal bread. Dolly found she enjoyed working with the dough. She didn't mind pitting and chopping cherries, blending ingredients, and felt fulfilled at the scent of baking, so much so that it almost seemed a spiritual experience.

Unaccountably, while she worked, Josh Frederick wasn't far from Dolly's thoughts. She wondered if he was learning as much about making wine in serene Napa Valley as she was about baking on the peaceful—if hectic during work hours—isle of Martha's Vineyard.

After moving from her more sumptuous accommodations, Dolly had settled into the tiny room at Blythe Cove Manor but found she hadn't needed much more than a bed and shower since she had to show up for work just after sunrise—borrowing a bike from Blythe to get there—and she worked twelve-hour days, surprised to still feel energized as she peddled back to the Manor. And Blythe had scores of books on the art of cooking and baking that Dolly devoured in the evenings before she fell into an exhausted sleep.

All too soon, summer was drawing to a close and once the tourists left the island, there'd be no more work for Dolly at the bakery. She'd been hired as summer help—and Marcie had made it clear from the start that she couldn't keep Dolly on past Labor Day. That was okay. Dolly had plenty of money—she didn't need a job. But the thought of leaving the island became almost too painful to bear. She'd fallen in love with the sunrises she saw from the window in her tiny room. She's grown to love the scent of the sea in the air—the sound of the foghorn that punctuated the nights and early mornings. The thought of returning to her old life and that lonely, empty condo totally repelled her.

And Marcie had mentioned on more than one occasion that she was thinking of retiring and selling the café. Could that be an opportunity for someone who had more than enough money to invest in a business? It was something Dolly wanted to contemplate.

And so it was on Labor Day morning that Dolly decided that it didn't matter if the tourists left the island and there was no work for her—she wasn't going to leave. Her heart had attached itself to Martha's Vineyard. She didn't need to worry about money—but she did need a place to live. Not something grand. Just a little house—and it didn't matter if it wasn't near the beach. She would contact a realtor and if she couldn't buy, maybe she could rent until she found something that would suit her. Not one of the massive cottages. She was, after all, just one person and without a lot of baggage—emotional or otherwise. But she supposed she should go home and figure out what she wanted and needed, and get rid of the rest—cut loose from a life she no longer felt a part of. And, not surprising, she didn't feel bad about it. She wanted to make a fresh start and the idea excited her.

Dolly tip-toed down the stairs so as not to disturb the Manor's other guests and wasn't at all surprised to find Blythe in the kitchen, baking yet another batch of her homemade muffins —cranberry this time.

"So, it's your last day on the job," Blythe commented as she pulled a pan of muffins from one of the Aga's ovens.

"Yes. I'm sad—but only because I won't get to learn any more from Marcie. She's been a wonderful instructor—and very generous in sharing her knowledge. I'm so grateful you got me the job."

"I didn't. I merely steered you toward it. You got it on your own. And from what Marcie tells me, she's sorry she couldn't keep you on."

"I understand. We talked about the financial problems of being a tourist destination and the harsh realities of staying afloat offseason. I think I judged Josh too harshly when we first met. I now understand why he feels he has to teach during the school year so he can afford to keep doing what he loves."

"Yes, he does need the teaching job—but he also loves it—and he's very good at it."

So Dolly had heard from a number of sources.

"Josh returned to the island just yesterday," Blythe said casually.

"Oh?" Dolly asked, trying not to sound all that interested, even if she *was* hungry to hear about his California adventure.

"He'll probably spend most of tomorrow setting up his class-room for the students, who go back to school on Wednesday."

"That's nice." Nice? Dolly hated to admit it, but she'd been counting the days until she could talk to him—quiz him about what he'd learned about wine during the preceding weeks. And she wondered if he'd undergone as profound a change as she had. Not only in her changed perceptions but physically, too. Pedaling to her temporary job had worked magic on her body. Despite tasting the baker's wares, Dolly had lost more than ten pounds while pedaling to work and felt better than she had in years.

Blythe nodded. "He gave me a call and asked about you."

Dolly raised an eyebrow. "Did he?"

Blythe transferred the muffins from the tray to a wire rack to finish cooling. "Would you like a cup of coffee and a muffin before you leave for work?"

"Sure. Could you spare a few moments to join me?"

"I'm sure I could."

"Great. Because I was hoping you could make another recommendation."

"A real estate agent?"

Dolly smiled. "Are you psychic?"

Blythe shook her head.

Dolly sighed wistfully. "Yeah. There's something about Martha's Vineyard...." But then she had no words to define the complex emotions she felt about the place.

Blythe didn't seem to need such an explanation. "I know," she said with just the hint of a smile. "I know."

The women looked out the big picture window that overlooked the gardens beyond. The morning light was different in early September compared to when Dolly had arrived a little more than a month before. And she marveled at how her life had changed in those short weeks.

"So, is Josh going to call me?" Dolly wondered aloud.

"Should I give him your cell number?" Blythe asked.

Dolly turned to her new friend and smiled. A world of possibilities was now open to her. "I wish you would."

Blueberry Cobbler
Ingredients
6 cups blueberries
⅓ cup granulated sugar
Zest of 1 large lemon
2 tablespoons light brown sugar
1 tablespoon cornstarch

<u>For the cobbler topping:</u>
2 cups all-purpose flour
2 teaspoons baking powder
½ teaspoon salt
½ cup granulated sugar
½ cup unsalted cold butter, cut into pieces
1 teaspoon vanilla extract
1 cup cold buttermilk
Heavy cream or milk, for brushing
Turbinado sugar, for sprinkling
vanilla ice cream (optional)
whipped cream (optional)

Preheat oven to 375ºF (190ºC, Gas Mark 5). Place the blueberries in a large bowl. In a small bowl, combine the granulated sugar and lemon zest. Rub together with your fingers until scented. Add the sugar-lemon mixture to the blueberries. Add the brown sugar and cornstarch. Gently stir until the blueberries are well coated. Let the mixture sit while you prepare the cobbler topping.

In a medium bowl, whisk together the flour, baking powder, salt, and sugar. Cut the cold butter into the flour mixture. Mix until the butter pieces are pea-sized. In a small bowl, whisk the cold buttermilk and vanilla together, then pour mixture into the dry ingredients. Stir with a spatula until the mixture comes together. Don't over-mix; the dough will be sticky.

Pour the blueberry mixture into a 9x13-inch pan. Drop pieces of the cobbler topping on top of the blueberries. Don't fret if there's space between the cobbler topping. Lightly brush the cobbler topping with heavy cream or milk. Sprinkle the turbinado sugar over the cobbler topping. Place the pan in the oven and bake for 45-50 minutes or until the cobbler topping is golden brown and the blueberries are bubbling. Remove from the oven and let cool on a wire rack for 15 minutes before serving. Serve with vanilla ice cream or whipped cream, if desired.

Note: Store cobbler, covered, in the refrigerator for 1-2 days. Can be reheated in the microwave.

Yield: 10 to 12 servings

Blueberry Crisp
<u>The filling</u>
Ingredients
4 cups blueberries (about a quart)
½ cup granulated sugar
juice and finely grated zest of 1 lemon
3 tablespoons all-purpose flour

<u>The topping</u>
Ingredients
½ cup butter
¾ cup firmly packed brown sugar
¾ cup quick cooking oatmeal
½ cup all-purpose flour
1 teaspoon ground cinnamon
whipped cream (optional)
vanilla ice cream (optional)

Preheat the oven to 350ºF (180ºC, Gas Mark 4). Butter a 13x9-inch baking pan. Combine the berries, sugar, lemon juice and zest, and flour in a large bowl.

Arrange the blueberry mixture in the baking pan. For the topping, melt the butter and stir in the sugar, oatmeal, flour, and cinnamon until well mixed. Sprinkle over the blueberries. Bake for 45 minutes until the crust is golden brown and the berries are soft. Serve warm with a dollop of whipped cream or a side of vanilla ice cream.

Yield: 8 to 10 servings

IF YOU ENJOYED ....

If you enjoyed **Grape Expectations** please consider spreading the word and reviewing it on your favorite online review site. Thank you!

Visit Lorraine's website
www.LorraineBartlett.com

FOUL WEATHER FRIENDS

A TALE FROM BLYTHE COVE MANOR

DESCRIPTION

Alone and suddenly single, Teagan Tate's visit to Martha's Vineyard for a previously planned couples weekend leaves her feeling more of a fifth wheel. And when the last ferry off the island is cancelled, she finds herself stranded in the middle of a nor'easter. Will the magic of Blythe Cove Manor and the kindness of two strangers help her find a new and happier life path?

CHAPTER 1

Teagan Tate sat in the back of the beat-up mini-van, watching snowflakes fly past her window.

"Looks like the weather's gettin' worse," said the driver who'd introduced himself as Ed.

It had been a quiet post-St. Patrick's Day weekend at Blythe Cove Manor on the island of Martha's Vineyard off the coast of Massachusetts. The B&B usually wasn't open during the first four months of the year but welcomed guests around some lesser winter holidays.

Teagan had been the fifth wheel between two other couples—her two besties from college and their husbands. The reservation had been made months before—before she and Jack had broken up right after New Year's because he'd decided their relationship was "too confining." Yeah, and he'd moved out of their apartment and in with another woman, someone he'd met at work—who was skinny, blonde, and spoke with the vocabulary of an eight-year-old.

Meow.

Teagan's besties, Kathryn and Lindy, had assured her she wouldn't feel at all uncomfortable during the getaway, but that hadn't been the case. Teagan just didn't feel like laughing and drinking too much wine during what had been billed as a couple's weekend. Instead, she'd spent way-too-many hours alone in her pretty room, working late into the night on her laptop on a project for work. She'd score points by delivering it early, and what else was there to do since there was no TV in any of the guest rooms. Because she'd stayed up so late, she'd over-slept and missed the early ferry that had whisked her friends away, which was why she was alone on that stormy Sunday afternoon.

"I'm supposed to pick up someone at the ferry. Hope he's up for the storm," Ed said.

Storm, schmorm. What was a little snow and wind? Okay, it meant the ocean would be turbulent. But then, it hadn't exactly been placid when Teagan had stepped onboard the ferry at Woods Hole two days before. Teagan was sure she could handle it. After all, what choice did she have? She had a bus to catch to get home to Connecticut to be at her job by eight the next morning.

Visibility wasn't good as the van traveled along the coast road and Ed slowed down on the parts that had already flooded. They were practically on top of the harbor before Teagan realized where they were. Through the heavy mist, she could see the big white lumbering ferry approach the dock and decided that March on the island wasn't the optimum time to visit. Maybe she'd make a return visit during the summer when the weather was fair, the trees were in leaf, and the fabulous gardens had all come back to life. But then, she wasn't sure she wanted to return alone. With Jack out of the picture....

The van pulled to a halt. "Uh-oh," Ed said.

"What's wrong?" Teagan asked.

He pointed to a flashing sign: SERVICE CANCELED DUE TO WEATHER.

"Oh no! I'm supposed to be back at work tomorrow morning," Teagan wailed.

"Sorry, lady, but it doesn't look like you're going to make it."

"What'll I do?"

"Like I said, I've got a reservation for someone coming in off that ferry. He's heading to Blythe Cove Manor. As this is offseason, I'm sure Ms. Calvert can put you up for a few more days until the storm passes and the ferries start running again."

"Yeah, but how am I going to pay for it?"

Ed merely shrugged.

Since Jack had left, and Teagan was paying the full cost of renting the apartment, it had stretched her budget to come to the island for the ill-fated weekend. What would it cost for her to stay at the Manor until she could escape and return home?

The windshield wipers whipped back and forth at a furious pace as the sleet seemed to grow in intensity. Ed tuned the van's radio to a local station, and they listened to the dour forecast as they waited for the ferry to dock.

Soon, several cars rolled off the big white ship, and they waited just a little longer until a few men and women, hunched against the elements, walked off the vessel, one of them—a man carrying a duffle and a small case—headed toward the van. Ed touched a button on his door's armrest to roll the driver's window down a few inches.

"You going to Blythe Cove Manor?" the man asked.

"Yeah." Ed got out and grabbed the guy's luggage. "Hop in." He walked around to the back of the van, letting in a great draft of icy air, placed the items next to Teagan's case, while the newcomer climbed in the front passenger seat.

The man turned to look at Teagan. "Hey, I didn't see you on the ferry. Are you're going to Blythe Cove Manor, too?"

"I was supposed to be leaving the island … until I saw the sign that the ferry service was calling it quits because of the storm," Teagan groused.

"Let me tell you, if I had a weak stomach, I'd have been puking my guts up after that wild ride."

"More information than I need to know," Teagan said sullenly.

"Sorry. I'm Adam Santos," he said by way of introduction.

"Teagan Tate. What brings you to Martha's Vineyard at this time of year?"

"Work."

Yeah—and now there was no way Teagan would make it to her place of employment the next morning.

Ed climbed back into the driver's seat, backed up the van, turned around, and off they went in the direction of Blythe Cove Manor.

"So was the journey across the sound an adventure?" Ed asked Adam with keen interest.

"More than a few people ran for the john for a barf-fest."

"Do we have to talk about vomit?" Teagan asked with disdain.

"I'm just saying how it was," Adam explained. "A couple of hysterical ladies seemed to think we might sink and drown before we reached the island."

"Not likely," Ed said offhandedly. "Those boats are as safe as a baby buggy but now we'll likely be cut off from the mainland for a few days. It's nothing we islanders can't handle."

Sure, that was easy for him to say—his job was *here* on the currently saturated hunk of rock and dirt. He could hunker down at home and not worry about his livelihood. Then again, his livelihood depended on people coming onto the Vineyard and carting them around. Maybe he had another job—or was retired —and taxi driving was just supplemental to his regular income.

Teagan looked out at the bleak, gray landscape and resisted the urge to cry. The entire weekend had been a bust. She should have forfeited the cancelation fee and just stayed home. And yet, despite the drawbacks, she had enjoyed her stay at Blythe Cove Manor, even with the shortcomings of spending so much time alone. Her room had exuded a feeling of calm and acceptance.

The public rooms felt warm and inviting, and the breakfasts had been hearty. The whole atmosphere reminded her of her childhood home where she'd felt valued and safe. Adulthood hadn't treated her as kindly.

But even home wasn't home anymore. Her siblings had scattered across the country, and her parents had followed her older brother to the Pacific Northwest. Because of that, she'd followed her college boyfriend back to Connecticut and far from her Arizona roots.

It snowed in the desert and was often just as cold as the northeast, but not relentlessly. Not for months and months on end. The weather in the southwest didn't wear down your soul in the early part of the year, although Teagan had to admit experiencing the changing of the seasons—the vibrancy of spring, the sultry summer days, and crisp fall evenings had come as a pleasant surprise. But even after six years in the Northeast, the winters seemed endless, bringing with them a sense of hopelessness. The dreary landscape around her was yet another reminder of that despair.

"What do you think, Teagan?" Adam asked.

Teagan shook the cobwebs from her mind. "Sorry. I was lost in thought. I haven't been following the conversation."

"That, because of the storm, the next few days could be an adventure."

Being stuck inside during a weather emergency when she could have been safe at home … in her lonely apartment.

"If you say so," she said wearily.

"And here we are," Ed said as the van pulled up the snow-covered, rutted drive that led to Blythe Cove Manor.

"Have you been here before?" Teagan asked Adam.

"No, but it was recommended to me by a friend. He said in winter I'd get a lot of work done because it's wicked dead around here."

"Ain't that the truth," Ed agreed with chagrin.

"So this is a working vacation?" Teagan asked.

"Sort of."

"What do you do?"

"I'm a software engineer and a writer. I'm working on a tech manual right now."

It sounded dreadfully dull. That said, Adam sure didn't look or sound like a typical IT geek, as evidenced by his interest in conversing.

Ed stopped the van in front of the inn and they all got out. Ed opened the back of the vehicle and redistributed the luggage. The travelers paid for the ride and then headed for the front doors with Teagan in the lead as the van took off.

"Welcome to Blythe Cove Manor. I'm your hostess, Blythe Calvert," the owner told Adam. "Welcome back, Teagan. I'm guessing the ferries have stopped running."

Teagan nodded.

Blythe addressed Adam again. "Won't you sign in?" She handed him a pen.

"Some weather you've got here," he said, sounding almost pleased, and signed the big old-fashioned ledger.

"Yes, well, I'm sorry to say that because of the weather, I can't offer you the cottage we spoke of when you first called."

"Oh?"

"It's likely the storm will take out the power."

"Does that happen often?"

"I'm afraid so. We can never predict when a nor'easter will hit, but this building has a generator. It can heat the entire structure, although it won't deliver electricity to most of the outlets in our guest rooms."

"Oh no," Teagan groaned. "We'll be living in the dark?"

"The kitchen, dining room, and our lobby/common area will have power should the grid go down, but I'm afraid that's all, but don't worry. I've got battery lanterns if we need them."

"As long as I can charge the battery on my laptop, I should be good to go," Adam said affably.

"Everything on the island, including the restaurants, will be shut down because of the storm, but I'll be offering additional meals at no extra charge," Blythe said.

Thank goodness for small mercies," Teagan thought.

"I'll serve a light supper in the dining room at seven."

"Thanks," Adam said.

"Thank you for understanding." Blythe turned her attention to Teagan. "You can have the same room you stayed in over the weekend or would you prefer another?"

Teagan sighed, her gaze dipping. "Staying here for a few more days wasn't in my budget. Do you have a cheaper room?"

"I'm sure we can make an arrangement about the bill," Blythe said.

What did that mean? That Teagan could pay it off in installments?

Blythe handed them both keys. "You're down the hall and to the left in the Sea Captain's room," she told Adam.

"I guess I know where I'm going," Teagan said.

The two guests headed toward the stairs, with Teagan mounting the steps while Adam inspected the doors to find his accommodation.

Upon entering her familiar room, Teagan could hear the wind, which seemed to have risen since she'd arrived back at the Manor just minutes before. She'd experienced more than a few nor'easters since her move to Connecticut, but never had she been so close to the sea to witness the full fury of such a storm. She knew the Manor had been around for at least two hundred years, so odds were it would withstand this storm, too, but she couldn't help but feel tendrils of worry creep up her spine.

Never had she felt so alone.

CHAPTER 2

The wind seemed to wail like a siren's song, but Teagan figured she'd better try to call her boss and leave a message to let her know she would be AWOL for a few days. Liz wouldn't be happy, but Teagan mentioned that she'd finished the Johnson project and hoped that would placate the woman. Would she have to take the time off as vacation? She'd find out upon her return to Connecticut.

After that, Teagan found a copy of a childhood favorite, Laura Ingalls Wilder's *The Long Winter* among the tomes on a small shelf in her room. Settling on the comfortable chair, with a lamp over her shoulder, she was soon lost in the story and read nearly half the book before her stomach growled and she ventured downstairs once again. After all, she'd had no lunch.

It was already dark and not long before dinner was to be served, and Teagan found herself alone in the B&B's lobby without even the resident cat for company. Since she'd arrived back at the inn, she noted the sleet had changed to snow and Teagan found herself drawn to the large floor-to-ceiling window that overlooked the patio and the sleeping garden beyond it. She had to stand up close to the glass and shield her eyes from the reflection to see the mesmerizing, swirling snow beyond.

On impulse, Teagan opened the nearby French doors that led to the patio which had been cleared of snow earlier in the day. Closing the door behind her, Teagan stood in the cold and dark, the wind-blown snowflakes swirling around her, her arms crossed to preserve her body warmth.

Despite the roar of the wind in her ears, Teagan thought she could hear the crash of waves in the cove below the bluff and could smell the tang of the sea. Had anyone ever leapt to their death from that precipice? What would drive someone to do such a thing?

Loneliness?

Maybe.

Could it be the lure of everlasting peace?

The idea both excited and frightened her—maybe because she suddenly realized that she'd been unhappy for a long, long time.

The door opened behind her.

"What are you doing out here?" Adam shouted from behind her, sounding concerned.

Teagan turned, feeling confused. "I don't know." Punishing herself? Yeah, maybe.

"Come back inside and get warm," he encouraged her, holding out a welcoming hand.

Teagan shrugged and followed him back into the inn's comforting warmth.

The gas fire blazed in the hearth giving the room a cozy feel. The night before it had also been lit as Kathryn, Lindy, and their husbands watched a comedy—drinking wine and eating buttered popcorn before Teagan had slunk back to her room to work ... and if she was honest, to brood.

"Supper will be served in a few minutes. As we're both on our own, we should probably sit together."

It seemed logical, so Teagan followed Adam to a table away from the windows and the darkness beyond.

"It's too bad we can't get a drink," Adam lamented.

"Oh, but we can have a glass of sherry. Ms. Calvert leaves a bottle and glasses out every evening," Teagan explained. She found said decanter on the dining room's sideboard, poured two glasses, and set them on the table before each of their places.

"Should we make a toast?" Adam asked.

"Why not?"

"To?"

It didn't take much to think of a topic. "Fair weather."

They clinked glasses and took sips of that fine sherry. Adam looked wistful.

"What's up?" Teagan asked.

He shook his head, but she thought she knew the reason for his thoughtful expression. If he had to be stranded, he would rather be stranded with someone other than a stranger. Yeah, well … she hadn't expected to be stranded, alone, either.

"Where are you from?" Adam asked conversationally.

"Now or where I grew up?"

"Both."

Teagan shrugged. "My parents were from Central Ohio, but Dad got a job in Phoenix and that's where I grew up. But I've been living in Connecticut since I graduated from college." She decided she wouldn't tell him why she'd landed there. "How about you?"

"Born and bred in Boston."

"But you don't have an accent."

"Not everybody does."

"And you became a tech writer because…?"

"I wrote the software. Nobody knows it like I do."

"What kind of software?"

"Diagnostic. I'm working with a 3-D x-ray developer. If we

can't beat cancer, we're going to be the best at treating it with radiography."

"Good for you. I wish you all the success in the world."

"Thanks. I got into this field because of my grandmother and her fight against the disease. She died, but if I can help other women live longer, it'll be in her honor."

Teagan smiled, realizing she'd taken a liking to Adam. "So, do you have a significant other?" she asked almost in jest.

He nodded. "Her name's Jamie. We're leaving for Ireland as soon as we sell our apartment."

Well, there went any thoughts of a storm-caused fling. Then again, he could have lied about his personal situation.

"How about you?"

"I'm floundering after being dumped," she answered honestly.

Adam shook his head. "The guy must have been a fool."

Teagan actually smiled. "You've got that right." She looked him in the eye and they both smiled. His was happy; hers reflective. "Why Ireland?"

"There are a lot of tech opportunities in Dublin. Besides, that's where my fiancée's people are from."

"And yours?"

"Originally from New Mexico."

"Not that far from Arizona."

"Not so far at all."

A noise from the kitchen drew their attention. Seconds later, Blythe called. "Ready for dinner?" She entered the dining room with a tray laden with bowls, a tureen, plates, and a small basket filled with what could only be homemade bread.

"Yes, ma'am," Adam said.

Blythe set the tray down on an adjacent table and doled out everything. "Help yourselves. And if you need anything, just call me."

"Thanks," Adam said and Teagan gave a grateful nod as well.

They plunged their spoons into what looked like New England clam chowder and sampled the soup.

"Wow. That's good," Adam said.

"Wait 'til you taste breakfast tomorrow," Teagan said, set her spoon down and reached for a piece of warm bread. The butter was soft and melted into what looked and smelled like sourdough. "What are the odds the power will go off?"

Adam took another spoonful of soup before answering. "I'd say it's a sure thing. I Googled nor'easters earlier this afternoon and I wouldn't be surprised if it goes out before we finish eating."

It was a self-fulfilling prophecy because suddenly the entire house was plunged into darkness for a full ten seconds before they heard the muffled sound of a generator firing up and the lights came back on.

"You must be psychic," Teagan teased.

Adam shrugged and continued eating.

"I guess we'll be stuck here for a couple of days," Teagan lamented.

"*You'll* be stuck. I'm booked for the week. As long as I can recharge my laptop's battery, it won't impact me much."

He was right. Since the library wouldn't have electrical outlets, would he hole up in his room to work as she had over the weekend, or would he set up a workstation on one of the dining room tables to be close to the amenities offered by the inn? She decided not to ask.

"What will you do for the next couple of days?" Adam asked.

Teagan shrugged. "Mope around here and feel sorry for myself, hoping I don't lose my job."

"You can't leave, so you may as well relax and enjoy yourself."

"Doing what?"

"Watch DVDs. I noticed there's a whole shelf of them by the big TV and there are a lot of books, too. You *do* read, don't you?"

"Of course I do. In fact, I read half a book just this afternoon." She didn't bother to mention it was a beloved children's book.

"But I didn't count on being stuck here. There's a real chance I could lose my job," she said.

"Do you like the job?"

She shook her head. "Not really."

"Then what will you lose?"

"My apartment, for one. My car for another." She sighed and set her spoon down, suddenly losing her appetite.

"What would you rather do instead?"

Teagan frowned. "That's a hard question. I mean ... I like working in public relations, but it's rather cut-throat—at least in our office."

"Is it something you could do online?"

"You mean start my own business?" Teagan asked.

"Why not?"

"Where would I find clients?"

"Surely you've made contacts during your career," he said and grabbed a piece of bread.

"A few," she admitted and picked up her spoon again, hoping her soup hadn't cooled too much. After all, she did need sustenance.

"You've already got a computer—that's about all you need."

"Oh yeah? What about stationery, business cards, pens, and pencils?"

"You can make your own stationery, and I'll bet you could scare up more than a dozen writing implements out of your kitchen junk drawer. Your biggest asset is your brain—*and* your experience. And think of all the money you'd save on clothes."

Teagan frowned. "I'd probably make up for it in gas to meet clients in neutral locations because I sure don't want to invite strangers into my home."

"Did you ever hear of renting workspace?" he offered.

Yes, she had ... but she'd never had to consider it before.

"There's nothing like working for yourself," Adam continued.

"You name your own hours, work in your pajamas if you want...." He took a big bite of bread, chewed and swallowed.

"I've also heard that entrepreneurs work a lot harder than being employed by the man—or woman," she added, thinking of her boss, Liz.

"That's true, but you only have to please yourself. And let me tell you, the old saying about doing what you love means you'll never work another day of your life is true."

This conversation was wearing Teagan down. "I wouldn't even know how to start."

"First, you start by beefing up your bank account. While you're doing that, you write a mission statement and start planning. That would give you a couple of months to get things set before you pull the plug on your nine-to-five job."

"You make it sound a little too easy."

"That's what I did. I'm happy in my work. I make a decent living, and I've never looked back."

So far. He was, after all, only in his thirties.

"You should think about it, and that's the last I'll say on the subject." He grinned. "At least for tonight."

Teagan sat back in her chair and eyed her dinner companion. Maybe he was cut out for a life on the edge, but she wasn't at all sure she could trust in a future with no safety net.

And yet ... what he'd described appealed to her. That said, she wasn't sure she had enough contacts to pull off starting a business. Could Liz and the agency come after her if she solicited customers from their list of clients? She wasn't sure.

No, no! The whole idea was pure nonsense.

Teagan grabbed the last piece of bread from the linen-lined basket and covered it with a thick layer of butter, taking a bite and chewing with defiance ... or was it defeat? At that moment, she wasn't quite sure.

THE HEARTH of the floor-to-ceiling fireplace was aglow with the steady flames of a gas fire flickering around faux wood. It wasn't being used to heat the expansive common room/lobby, but it gave the room a cozy feel—something Teagan hadn't felt on the previous two nights of her stay here at the Manor. Her friends and their spouses seemed to suck up all the energy in the space and she'd been content to leave them and go back to her room to work.

As she watched the dancing flames, Teagan wondered where Blythe Cove Manor's generator resided. She'd taken a walk along the beach below the bluff the previous morning, gaining access via a long set of stairs but hadn't seen the mighty machine on her journey. When she thought about it, that walk by the sea had been her favorite part of her visit to Blythe Cove. There was something about the sea, wild and dangerous as it was, that attracted her. She liked the salty tang in the air—the ocean's unpredictability. She'd found several different shells and pocketed a few as souvenirs, because despite the whole debacle of a weekend, she'd wanted to remember her time on Martha's Vineyard. She felt a strong attraction to the island and she wasn't quite sure why.

"So, what do you want to play?" Adam asked, standing in front of a tall bookshelf that held a number of board games. "*Monopoly, Chutes and Ladders,* or *Candyland?*"

"Are you kidding me? *Chutes and Ladders* and *Candyland?*"

"Okay, I *was* kidding with those two. But we could also play Parcheesi, checkers, or chess."

"I've never played Parcheesi, and I'd be bored by checkers, so chess it is," Teagan said.

Adam raised an eyebrow but didn't comment. Instead, he pulled the box from the shelf and brought it over to the big chest that served as a coffee table before the big leather sofa. He sat down and set up the board before holding out his hands, with two pieces hidden in his cupped palms. "Ladies first—you get to choose."

Teagan pointed toward his left hand. He presented the chess piece: white. Teagan smiled, replaced the piece on the board at the same time he did, and reached for the pawn in front of her king, moving it forward.

"So, tell me all about yourself," Adam said as he, too, moved a pawn.

"There's not much to tell."

"You came here to Martha's Vineyard on your own?"

Teagan moved one of her knights. "Sort of. I met some friends here at Blythe Cove Manor. They left on the early ferry—I kind of … overslept."

"I'll say." He moved another pawn. "I'm surprised they didn't call you."

"I'd been working on a project for my job and I guess they figured I'd just catch the next ferry back to the mainland."

"Knowing that a storm was brewing?" he asked, sounding surprised.

"Yeah, I kind of thought the same thing," she admitted, her disappointment weighing on her soul.

"Where did you meet these people?"

"College."

"You went to school in the East?"

She nodded. "I got a scholarship to Smith. After graduation, I stayed in the area—relatively speaking." She moved another piece.

Adam studied the board. "No boyfriend?"

"Not anymore."

He looked up. "Sore subject?"

Teagan shrugged. "Not really."

"That's what you say; your eyes tell a different story."

Okay, so it wasn't the truth, but she wasn't sure she wanted to spill said story to Adam—a virtual stranger—so she said nothing.

"It's okay. We've all been dumped."

"But you're with a wonderful woman and you're going to move to Ireland and go on a brand new adventure." She hoped she didn't sound as bitter as she felt.

He didn't seem to notice. "Yeah. We're looking forward to it. What're your plans for the future?" he asked and moved his bishop.

"Get up, go to work. Lather, rinse, repeat." She moved one of her pawns forward again.

"That doesn't sound like much fun."

"It isn't."

"And you're worried about losing that crummy job?"

"It keeps a roof over my head. But I will admit I was intrigued by your suggestions over dinner."

"I'm flattered." Another of his pawns advanced. "Say you did work for yourself, would you stay in New England?"

Teagan looked up, startled by the question. "I—I don't know." She shrugged. "I guess there's no reason why I'd have to. Except moving is expensive."

"We're selling or donating just about everything we own. We figure this is the chance of a lifetime and we're not going to let material things keep us from doing what we want. Besides, between Craigslist and thrift shops, why pay retail for anything? I'm also into upcycling," he added.

Teagan couldn't help herself. For the first time that weekend, she actually laughed.

A gust of wind so fierce hit the old building so hard it seemed to shake. Teagan shivered, wishing she'd packed a heavier sweater. As it was, she had run out of clean underwear. After all, she'd only packed for a two-day stay. She would have to wash her lingerie in her bathroom sink and hope her deodorant really was as strong as a man's though made for a woman. And even though the generator kept the inn warm, a chill seemed to have encircled her heart. She also knew that she'd felt that way since the day Jack left her.

She noticed Adam studying her.

"Are you okay?" he asked.

She shook her head. "Not really. I guess I'm a little fragile."

"Like a soap bubble?" he suggested.

She smiled. "Okay, not *that* fragile. I'm trying to figure out where I belong in the world."

Suddenly, the Manor's resident cat jumped onto Teagan's lap. She hadn't even been aware that Martha had been anywhere nearby. "Hey, pretty kitty." She stroked the cat's soft fur, and Martha instantly began to purr.

"That cat likes you," Adam observed.

Teagan couldn't help but smile. "When I was a kid, we always had cats. My folks still have my cat, Barney, with them in Washington."

"I take it you don't have any pets right now," Adam stated.

Teagan shook her head. "Jack was allergic to any kind of pet dander. Maybe that's why he—" She didn't elaborate. Maybe if Jack had had a pet growing up he might have grown up to be a kinder, gentler man.

Maybe.

"Check," Adam said, disturbing Teagan's reverie.

Squinting, she examined the board considering her next move. Then she lifted her king. "Checkmate."

Incredulous, Adam studied the board. "Damn. Why didn't I see that coming?"

Teagan smiled. "Maybe you were preoccupied."

Adam scowled. "Or maybe I just wasn't paying attention."

Or maybe Teagan was just a better chess player. She wasn't about to voice that opinion.

"Another game?" Adam asked.

The wind howled yet again.

Teagan stroked the cat's fur. "I don't think so."

"Then how about another sherry before we turn in for the night?" he asked.

Martha gave a cheerful *bluurpt* and the two humans laughed. "Why not?" Teagan said.

Adam got up and retrieved the decanter from the dining room sideboard and refilled their glasses.

Martha looked up at Teagan. The forceful wind didn't frighten the cat, who seemed perfectly content to be petted or have her warm ears rubbed.

Teagan leaned back into the sofa's warm leather and felt herself relax. Despite the storm, a sense of peace descended upon her. Like the cat, she somehow knew she was safe here at Blythe Cove Manor.

The sound of the wind never really bothered Teagan. Even in the desert, she somehow found a wailing storm to be reminiscent of a song. It should have frightened her. Strong winds could be deadly and destructive, but oddly enough she believed they would never hurt her. It was a stupid assumption, but she couldn't shake that feeling.

The relentless gale must have howled throughout the night, but Teagan had only awakened twice. The first time, after a dream. She'd stood on the shore of an island but it looked nothing like she'd seen on her visit to Martha's Vineyard. She watched the sun sink into the horizon as a voice called from somewhere behind her. *"What are you waiting for?"*

The second time, she'd awoken, the wind was the cause. Teagan was glad she'd left the battery-operated lantern her hostess had given her alight, finding its glow a comfort, and had easily drifted back to sleep. Still, the next morning she was up before sunlight broke over the island.

After a quick wash, she dressed and wandered downstairs, she tiptoed through the lobby/common room area and could see lights in the kitchen beyond. "Hello," she called so as not to startle her hostess.

"Good morning, Teagan," Blythe said.

Teagan entered the brightly lit kitchen. She could still hear the muffled roar of the generator, so she knew that power had not yet been restored to the island, but she could also smell the heavenly aroma of something delicious baking in the big ivory-colored AGA cooker that took up a considerable amount of real estate in that kitchen.

"What're you baking?" Teagan asked.

"Blueberry muffins. I picked the berries myself last fall."

"Smells heavenly."

"Of course, you and Adam can have just about anything you want for breakfast. I don't usually have such an open-ended menu, but these are unusual circumstances."

A particularly loud gust of wind shook the building once more. The women looked at each other and Teagan gave a nervous laugh. "Do you ever worry about these storms?"

Blythe shook her head and gave a knowing smile. "The core of this house was built over two centuries before I was born. I have no doubt it will be here two centuries after I'm gone."

"That must comfort you."

"It does." She changed the subject. "Did you sleep all right?" Blythe asked, her concern genuine.

"Better than I would have thought. Going back to my room was like a warm welcome home." She shrugged, feeling embarrassed. "I know that sounds stupid, but—"

"Not at all," Blythe assured her.

"I woke up a couple of times but went right back to sleep. I dreamed about the ocean." "Funny thing is … it wasn't here on Martha's Vineyard. At least, I don't think so. There were waves gently lapping against a sandy beach and a beautiful sunset."

The timer on the cooker rang and Blythe grabbed two potholders before pulling the tray of piping hot muffins from one of the ovens and placing them on top of the cooktop. A wire rack stood nearby as the staging ground for the purple-stained confections.

"What would you like to drink? Tea, coffee, or hot chocolate?" Blythe asked.

Though not a bit chilled, Teagan felt warmed through by the thought of grasping a big mug of cocoa. "Hot chocolate."

"I think I'll join you ... if you don't mind."

"I'd like that," Teagan said and smiled. There was something unusual about Blythe Cove Manor's hostess that conveyed a sense of comfort and trust ... reminding Teagan just a little of her grandmother, though Blythe was decades younger than her Nana had been when she'd died.

Blythe removed the muffins from their metal prison and set them on the rack to further cool, then set about to make cocoa. Teagan watched in amused fascination.

With the mugs and muffins on a tray, Blythe led the way to the lobby/common room instead of stopping at one of the dining room's tables. She set the tray on the big chest that served as a coffee table and gestured for Teagan to sit before she took her seat on the other side of the big leather couch.

Once again the gas fire was ablaze, lending the room an atmosphere of warmth, security, and comfort.

Blythe gestured toward the tray. "Help yourself."

Teagan picked up a muffin and peeled off the paper wrapper. She took a bite of the still-warm delight and gave a sigh of pure pleasure. "This has to be *the* best muffin I've ever tasted. What's your secret?"

Blythe shrugged but then gave a coy smile. "It's said that the fairies and brownies that live here on the island tend our gardens. Who am I to dispute that?"

Fairies? Brownies? No matter; the muffin was delicious.

Once again the wind seemed to rattle the rafters making Teagan give an involuntary shudder.

"Do storms unnerve you?" Blythe asked.

"No. But … there's something niggling at the back of my brain. I didn't feel it over the weekend when I was here with my friends, but since they've gone and I had to return … something seems different."

"In what way?"

Teagan wasn't sure how to answer. "When I was with them, I felt like an afterthought. Like I wasn't a part of the experience. But since I returned after leaving yesterday afternoon, it's been a totally different experience."

"Maybe you had expectations when you first arrived that could never be fulfilled," Blythe suggested, and then took a bite of her own muffin.

Teagan nodded. "That's for sure. As you know, my reservation was supposed to be for two. And I appreciate that you changed the payment tier when I showed up alone."

"It was the least I could do."

"Well, I just want you to know how much I appreciate it."

"You're welcome."

The women ate their muffins and sipped their cocoa in companionable silence until the wind once again fiercely gusted around the inn.

"How long do you think the storm will last?" Teagan asked.

"Through the day … maybe until tomorrow. But then … maybe not. You never know. A nor'easter is totally unpredictable."

Not unlike the rest of life.

"I don't really know much about nor'easters, except that they're big storms that can hang around for days."

"And they can happen in warmer weather, too," Blythe said.

"Is this a private party?" came a voice from behind the women.

"Please join us," Blythe said and stood. "We're having blueberry muffins and cocoa. Can I get you a mug?"

"If it's not too much trouble."

"Not at all."

Blythe rose, picked up her own mug and plate, and headed for the kitchen. Adam sat down on the chair nearest Teagan.

"Boy, this storm is relentless. I woke up in the night and swore the wind would rip off the roof."

Teagan giggled. "And I slept like a baby."

Blythe returned with another tray and set down the cocoa and muffin in front of Adam. "What else would you two like for breakfast?"

"After that muffin, I'm not sure I need anything else," Teagan said.

"I'll hold off judgment until after I've eaten mine," Adam said good-naturedly.

"I thought about making grilled cheese for lunch," Blythe said. It seemed a rather pedestrian meal, but then she wasn't charging extra to feed them Teagan reminded herself. "I'll let you two chat. I've got to feed my cat."

Teagan hadn't seen Martha that morning, but sure enough, the cat seemed to have just appeared from nowhere and gave a sharp, *"Meow!"* as if in agreement. They watched their hostess retreat to the kitchen once again.

"What have you got planned for the day?" Adam asked as he peeled the paper wrapper from his muffin.

Teagan shrugged. "I thought I might set my laptop up in the dining room and work up another work project."

"Same here. After all, that's why I came to the island —to work."

Teagan drank the last of her cocoa. The sky outside the French doors was becoming a dull gray, and snow still swirled out on the patio. She glanced around the cozy room. If she had to be stranded somewhere during a fierce storm, she couldn't imagine a better place.

CHAPTER 4

Teagan brought her laptop down to the dining room and set it up, glad she'd thought to recharge the battery before going to bed the night before the storm hit. She opened her files and had been working for about ten minutes when Adam joined her.

"Do you mind if I set up on the same table?"

"Be my guest," Teagan said and gestured toward the chair opposite her. Soon the two were busy working and Teagan became so engrossed in her project that she didn't even notice the storm raging outside.

It was nearly noon when Adam stood and stretched, then turned to look out the window. The sky had brightened, but the wind had not abated. "I sure could go for a walk."

"You mean you'd *like* to go for a walk. I wouldn't advise it right now."

Adam reclaimed his chair. "I came here to work, but I also thought I might see a little of the island. At least try dinner at The Black Dog Tavern in Vineyard Haven. I heard they're open year round."

"We went there on Saturday night."

"Was that the highlight of your weekend?"

Teagan shook her head. "The food was great. The company was … okay."

"Did you have time to see much of the island?" Adam asked.

Again Teagan shook her head. "Most of it is shut down in winter. I wanted to check out the house of a famous cookbook author who lives here, but the opportunity didn't present itself."

"How are you when it comes to cooking?"

"Not bad, but my ex was a junk-food junkie. His idea of eating healthy was a side of French fries with every meal. He wouldn't eat a green vegetable to save his life."

Adam's expression darkened. Was he judging her by her choice of lover? "Jamie and I cook together often."

"It must be fun."

"Yeah. Once we get to Ireland, we're hoping to have a vegetable garden. If we don't rent a home with a yard, we'll rent an allotment to grow some of our own food."

"I've always wanted to have a real garden. Except for cactus, not much grows in the Arizona desert," Teagan said. "My brother and his family live on Bainbridge Island on Puget Sound across from Seattle, and they have an amazing garden."

"You've been there?"

"Just once."

"And how was it?"

Teagan smiled. "Wonderful."

"I hear the weather is kind of gloomy." At that moment, the wind howled particularly loudly.

"And this is better?" Teagan asked.

Adam laughed. "I guess not. But we only have a few nor'easters a year. I heard it rains in Seattle over a hundred and fifty days of the year."

"So my brother said, but he loves it there. He'd rather have rain than desert heat."

"What about you?"

"What?"

"Would you rather have the rain and your family than live here on the East Coast?"

Teagan shrugged. "I hadn't given it a thought."

"Maybe you should."

Teagan's gaze dipped to her keyboard. Why *hadn't* she considered moving west to be closer to her family after breaking up with Jack?

"Excuse me," came a voice from the kitchen entrance. Blythe held a large silver tray. "Luncheon is served." She headed for a table near the window overlooking the patio and set down the tray, then she emptied it, first placing a soup tureen in the center, and then plates with large grilled-cheese sandwiches garnished with pickle slices on the side, but the sandwiches were unlike anything Teagan had ever seen.

"Blueberry grilled cheese?" she asked, confused.

"*Balsamic* blueberry grilled cheese sandwiches on sourdough bread. I hope you like them."

"I'm up for trying anything new—and I love blueberries," Adam said, moving closer to the table where Teagan joined him.

"Please sit and serve yourselves," Blythe said, picking up the tray and returning to the kitchen.

They took their seats and Teagan picked up a ladle to dole out portions of soup for both of them. It was another batch of Blythe's wonderful clam chowder. Adam bent closer and examined the golden brown sandwich halves. He lifted one, took a sniff, then bit into it and moaned, chewing.

"Good?" Teagan asked.

"Mmm-hmm," he managed before swallowing. "Wow—that is *different*."

Teagan sampled one of her halves and blinked in surprise. Totally unexpected, and totally delicious. "I never would have thought of pairing blueberries with cheese."

"Don't forget the vinegar. That gives it a nice tang," Adam agreed.

"What kind of cheese do you think this is?"

"Havarti?" He took another bite. "Definitely Havarti and probably mozzarella."

"Ms. Calvert told me she picked the blueberries she uses in her cooking."

"Mmm," Adam managed, his mouth full of sandwich. He chewed and swallowed. "I'm sorry to have missed going to some of the local eateries, but I sure can't complain about the food here at the Manor. I wonder if Ms. Calvert gives cooking lessons."

"She's got one of those big English stoves. I'll bet it takes some getting used to. It doesn't have regular burners."

"Maybe she'd show us how it works."

They talked about cooking and their favorite recipes until they'd finished eating and Blythe returned to clear away the dishes.

"Can I do anything to help?" Teagan asked. "I can wash dishes, or at least load a dishwasher."

"Thanks, but I can manage," Blythe said with a smile.

"We were wondering if you'd be willing to show us how your stove works. Teagan says it's not like a typical range."

"The AGA does take a bit of getting used to, but now that I've had it a while, it's second nature to me—and I love the multiple ovens. When you bake as much as I do, it's a godsend. I'd be delighted to show you how it works. I'll let you know when I'm ready to start dinner so I can tell you all about it."

"Would you like some help making dinner?" Teagan asked.

"Would you mind chopping vegetables?"

"I happen to excel at that," Adam said.

"Me, too," Teagan said.

"Thank you. I think it would be fun," Blythe said, picking up the last of the dishes before heading back to the kitchen.

Adam gave Teagan a smile and then heaved a sigh as his gaze

returned to the window and the gray landscape beyond. "I need to get back to work."

Teagan nodded and watched as he returned to the table they'd established as their workstation, then she turned her attention back out the window, lingering to watch the storm. There wasn't much to see except the snow being blown around the patio, and her mind wandered back to hers and Adam's earlier conversation. What *could* she do to make the move to the West Coast?"

Teagan was pretty sure her family would welcome her back with open arms. They'd lamented the fact that she'd elected to stay in the east after she'd graduated from college. As she considered her options, Teagan realized she could probably sell the bulk of her possessions and ship everything else. She could probably even set up possible job interviews via Skype.

It could work, but first, she needed to plan—not just for a move, but do as Adam suggested and write a mission statement for both scenarios.

Teagan stood and returned to her workstation, created a new document, and began to type.

IT WAS LATE in the afternoon when Adam stood and stretched, drawing Teagan's attention. He turned to look outside. "Hey, I think the wind has died down."

Sure enough, the snow was no longer pelting the Manor. Instead, the flakes seemed to be dancing. And although the wind had subsided, the sky was still steel gray.

Adam ducked his head and sported a sly grin. "Have you ever built a snowman?"

"Not since college. My roommates and I built one outside our dorm. We gave him a beret, a scarf, carrot nose, and sticks for arms, but the poor snowman was blind because we didn't have anything to give him eyes."

"In the purest sense, a snowman doesn't need any of that. Just three big snowballs in diminishing sizes." Adam's grin widened. "How about we build one now?"

"Are you serious?" Teagan asked.

"Why not?"

Teagan thought it over. "No reason I can think of."

A minute later they'd donned their coats, hats, scarfs, gloves, and in Teagan's case, boots. The air was bitterly cold, but within minutes they had formed the snowman's large base and set about making the next big giant snowball for the middle. Teagan found herself laughing as they struggled to put the second ball onto the first and realized she hadn't had as much fun in a long, long time.

When the snowman was complete, she removed her scarf and tied it around its neck. "There, now you won't freeze."

"It's *you* who's going to freeze," Adam pointed out. "If he gets warm, he's toast."

"More like a puddle of water."

The wind had picked up, blowing the scarf until it whipped around the snowman's face.

Adam looked overhead. The sky appeared to be darkening. "Looks like the break in the storm is over. We'd better get back inside before we get blown over."

They trudged back through the snow and reentered the Manor.

"That's where you are," Blythe said. "I came looking for you to help with dinner—that is, if you're still interested."

"I am," Teagan said.

"So am I," Adam echoed. He glanced at his watch. "I didn't realize it was so late."

"That's daylight savings time for you," Teagan quipped.

The two of them hung up their coats and regrouped in the Manor's charming kitchen where Blythe gave them a quick tutorial on how her AGA cooker operated.

"What are we going to make?" Adam asked.

"Chicken stew. It's an easy recipe and it's quite filling. I've cleaned the vegetables, now if you two could just chop them for me, I'll get the chicken started."

They talked as they chopped, and once all the prep was done, Blythe added the vegetables and broth to the other ingredients and Teagan and Adam placed the cutting boards and knives in the sink. "And now we let it cook for about twenty minutes. Perhaps you'd like to retire to the common room for a pre-dinner sherry," Blythe suggested.

"That doesn't seem fair," Teagan said. "You're doing all the work tending the dish."

"And you are my guests," Blythe said with a sincere smile. "I'll call you when dinner is ready."

Teagan and Adam left the kitchen to return to the common room. Once again, Teagan took a seat on the comfortable couch while Adam poured the sherry and brought it over. He handed her a glass before taking a seat on the opposite end of the sofa. "You were working pretty intently this afternoon. Did you finish your project for work?"

"No. In fact, I was trying to figure out how to get *out* of working."

Adam's brow furrowed. "Excuse me?"

Teagan eased off her shoes and drew her legs up, folding them under her. "You really got me thinking yesterday; what is it I want out of life?"

"And you came up with the answer?" he asked and sipped his drink.

She nodded. "I think so. I started thinking about my home— or the lack of it."

He raised an eyebrow.

"I realized my apartment isn't a home. It never really was. And now that I'm there alone, it's just a place to eat dinner, sleep, and then get up the next morning and do it all again. I want more out of life than that."

"And have you figured out what that more is?"

"I think so. I want to go *home*."

"But I thought you said you didn't *have* a home base anymore."

"I thought about that, and I realized that my home is where my family is. And my folks and my brother and his family are in Washington. That's where I want to go."

"Are you sure you want to make that kind of an adjustment?"

Teagan shrugged. "While staying here at Blythe Cove Manor, I've felt a sense of peace. I don't know if it's just the hospitality of Blythe Cove Manor, or …."

"Or what?"

She thought about her answer for long seconds before speaking. "It's the ocean. The sound of it. The tang."

"The Atlantic is a lot more volatile than the Pacific," Adam pointed out.

"All the better."

"It couldn't have been just my talking about it that changed your mind."

She shrugged. "Maybe I had to come to Blythe Cove Manor to learn where I need to be. It wasn't here on Martha's Vineyard, but on *an* island across the country with my parents, my brother, and his family. I want to spend my holidays and free time with the people I love the most."

Adam raised his glass. "Then let's toast to your new adventure."

Teagan raised her glass.

"To the move."

They clinked glasses.

CHAPTER 5

Over dinner, Teagan quizzed Adam, asking him to list all the steps he and his fiancée had undertaken to downsize their possessions and get ready for their move overseas. Before she fell asleep that evening, Teagan had added his suggestions to her already lengthy list of things to do.

Making such a monumental decision felt good. It felt right.

It was long overdue.

And, oddly enough, upon climbing into bed, Teagan fell into a deep, restful sleep.

The storm raged for another two days and nights, but by Thursday morning, Teagan peered through the curtains of her room to witness the sun rise in a clear, chilly blue sky. The storm was over and she was delighted to find the power had already been restored. She took a leisurely shower, dressed, and was downstairs at precisely eight o'clock to find Adam seated at one of the tables, already working.

"Hey," he said, looking up. "The internet is back—and I got a cell signal. I've already spoken to Jamie. She was worried when she couldn't reach me for a couple of days."

"I should go get my phone to see if anyone has tried to get a hold of me, too," Teagan said and marched back up the stairs. She retrieved her phone and found there were several text messages —all of them from her mother, but none, she noticed, from her so-called besties who'd left the island five days before.

Teagan knew her mother usually left her phone in the kitchen to charge overnight, so didn't feel any qualms about sending a quick message to say she was okay and would call later. She set her phone down on the dresser and left her room, but no sooner had she taken a step when she heard her ringtone sound.

She hurried back to her room, sat on her bed, and quickly tapped the answer-call icon.

"Teagan?"

"Mom? What are you doing up so early?"

"I've been worried sick that I couldn't reach you. I haven't slept in days."

"Oh, Mom, I'm so sorry. I'm at a B&B on Martha's Vineyard. Because of the storm, I couldn't get a cell signal. I'm okay and I'm so sorry you and Dad had to worry."

"I'm just thankful you're okay, baby."

"I am … and I want you to be the first to know that being here has given me a new perspective."

"And that is?" her mother asked, sounding almost stern.

"That I thought I might relocate to the Seattle area. What do you think about that?"

"Ever since you broke up with Jack, I've been wondering … what are you waiting for?"

Teagan thought back to her dream days before and realized that the voice who'd spoken to her had been her mother's. "I'm sorry it took so long. But I met two wonderful people here whose wisdom brought me to that conclusion."

"I'd love to hear all about it," Teagan's mother said.

And so, Teagan told her mother of her plans for the future.

"Don't worry, baby, your family will be here—ready and willing to welcome you back with open arms."

Teagan smiled. She was finally going home.

THE FOURTH of July holiday always meant a packed house at Blythe Cove Manor, with sunny skies, the garden ablaze with color, and the blueberry bushes festooned with fruit that's not quite ready for picking, but full of the promise of pies, cobblers, and more to come.

Most of the guests were away from the Manor, sunning themselves on beaches, eating ice cream cones, and having lobster lunches when Blythe walked down the sandy, rutted drive to the mailbox. Getting mail was always a surprise. Packages, letters, and the inevitable bills could arrive on any given day.

As she sorted through the envelopes, a colorful postcard popped to the surface. It was of the Seattle space needle. Written in green ink were the words, "Glad I came here. Teagan Tate."

Blythe smiled. Another one touched by the magic of Blythe Cove Manor.

As she walked back to the Manor, Blythe decided to use part of the remaining package of last year's blueberries to make her lunch: a balsamic blueberry grilled-cheese sandwich, and then a batch of muffins.

She was having a very good day.

Blythe's Easy Clam Chowder
Ingredients
4 slices bacon, diced
2 tablespoons unsalted butter
2 cloves garlic, minced
1 onion, diced
½ teaspoon dried thyme
3 tablespoons all-purpose flour
1 cup milk
1 cup vegetable stock
2 6.5-ounce cans chopped clams, juice reserved
1 bay leaf
2 russet potatoes, peeled and diced
1 cup half and half
Kosher salt and freshly ground black pepper, to taste
2 tablespoons chopped fresh parsley leaves

Heat a large stockpot or Dutch oven over medium-high heat. Add the bacon and cook until brown and crispy, about 6-8 minutes. Transfer to a paper towel-lined plate, reserving 1 tablespoon excess fat; set aside. Melt butter in the stockpot. Add the garlic and onion, and cook, stirring frequently, until the onions have become translucent, about 2-3 minutes. Stir in the thyme until fragrant; about 1 minute. Whisk in the flour until lightly browned, about 1 minute. Gradually whisk in the milk, vegetable stock, clam juice, and bay leaf, and cook, whisking constantly until slightly thickened; about 1-2 minutes. Stir in the potatoes.

Bring to a boil; reduce heat and simmer until potatoes are tender; about 12-15 minutes.*

Stir in half and half and clams until heated through, about 1-2 minutes; season with salt and pepper, to taste. If the soup is too thick, add more half and half as needed until desired consistency is reached. Serve immediately. Garnished with bacon and parsley, if desired.

Yield: 3-4 serving

Blueberry Streusel Muffins
Ingredients
1½ cups all-purpose flour
2¾ teaspoons baking powder
¾ teaspoon salt
½ cup granulated sugar
2 teaspoons grated lemon rind
1 large egg, lightly beaten
¾ cup milk
⅓ cup vegetable oil (or unsweetened applesauce)
1 cup fresh or frozen blueberries thawed and drained
1 tablespoon all-purpose flour
1 tablespoon sugar
¼ cup granulated sugar
2½ tablespoons all-purpose flour
½ teaspoon ground cinnamon

1½ tablespoons butter

Preheat the oven to 400ºF (200ºC, Gas Mark 6). In a large mixing bowl, combine the flour, baking powder, salt, sugar and lemon rind. In a small bowl, combine the egg, oil (or applesauce) Make a well in the dry ingredients and pour in the wet mixture, stirring until moistened. Combine the blueberries, 1 tablespoon of flour and 1 tablespoon of sugar, tossing gently to coat. Fold the blueberry mixture into the batter. Using a small ice cream scoop (or spoon) put the batter into a paper-cup lined muffin tin. Fill to the ¾ point. For the streusel: combine ¼ cup sugar, 2½ tablespoons flour, and cinnamon. Cut in the butter until crumbly. Bake for 18 minutes or until golden.

Yield: 12 muffins

Balsamic Blueberry Grilled-Cheese Sandwich
Ingredients
4 slices of sourdough bread
Butter
A good amount of white cheeses (any combination of Havarti, Mozzarella, Monterey, Swiss, or Sharp White Cheddar)
Fresh spinach or arugula
½ cups fresh or frozen blueberries
1 tablespoon balsamic vinegar
1½ teaspoons brown sugar

In a small saucepan, combine the blueberries, sugar, and vinegar. Turn on medium heat and let come to a slow boil. Use a muddler or other utensil to crush berries as you stir. After boiling for about 5 minutes, pour the mixture into a mesh strainer and let the syrup separate from the solid berries. (Save the syrup for another purpose.) Butter one side of two slices of bread. Spread the blueberries onto the unbuttered sides of the bread, top with cheese, some spinach, then more cheese. Sprinkle with freshly ground pepper. Top with the other slices of bread and grill in a greased skillet until browned.

Yield: 2 sandwiches

Blythe's Easy Chicken Stew
  Ingredients
  ⅓ cup all-purpose flour
  ½ teaspoon salt
  Dash of pepper
  1½ pounds boneless skinless chicken breasts, cut into 1-inch
pieces
  3 tablespoons butter
  1 medium onion, sliced
  3 celery stalks, sliced
  2 medium potatoes, peeled and cut into ¾-inch cubes
  3 medium carrots, cut into 1/4-inch slices
  1½ cups chicken broth
  ½ teaspoon dried thyme
  1½ tablespoon cornstarch

In a large resealable plastic bag, combine the flour, salt, and pepper. Add the chicken, a few pieces at a time, and shake to coat. In a large skillet, melt the butter; cook the chicken until the juices to run clear. Add the onion and celery and cook for 3 minutes. Stir in the potatoes and carrots. In a small bowl, combine the broth, thyme, and cornstarch; stir into the skillet. Bring to a boil. Reduce the heat; cover and simmer for 15 to 20 minutes or until the vegetables are tender.

Yield: 4 to 6 servings

IF YOU ENJOYED...

If you enjoyed *Foul Weather Friends*, and in fact all of Mystical Blythe Cove Manor, please consider spreading the word and reviewing it on your favorite online review site. Thank you!

Find Lorraine on Social Media
www.LorraineBartlett.com

ABOUT THE AUTHOR

The immensely popular Booktown Mystery series is what put Lorraine Bartlett's pen name Lorna Barrett on the New York Times Bestseller list, but it's her talent--whether writing as Lorna, or L.L. Bartlett, or Lorraine Bartlett—that keeps her in the hearts of her readers. This multi-published, Agatha-nominated author pens the exciting Jeff Resnick Mysteries as well as the acclaimed Victoria Square Mystery series, the Tales of Telenia adventure-fantasy saga, and now the Lotus Bay Mysteries, and has many short stories and novellas to her name(s). Check out the descriptions and links to all her works, and sign up for her emailed newsletter here: http://oi.vresp.com/?fid=aee11a8d64

If you enjoyed *MYSTICAL BLYTHE COVE MANOR,* please consider reviewing it on your favorite online review site. Thank you!

Find Lorraine on Social Media
www.LorraineBartlett.com

facebook.com/LorraineBartlettAuthor

twitter.com/LorraineBartlet

instagram.com/bartlett_lorraine

pinterest.com/LorraineBartlet

ALSO BY LORRAINE BARTLETT

THE LOTUS BAY MYSTERIES

Panty Raid (A Tori Cannon-Kathy Grant mini mystery)

With Baited Breath

Christmas At Swans Nest

A Reel Catch

The Best From Swans Nest (A Lotus Bay Cookbook)

THE VICTORIA SQUARE MYSTERIES

A Crafty Killing

The Walled Flower

One Hot Murder

Dead, Bath and Beyond (with Laurie Cass)

Yule Be Dead (with Gayle Leeson)

Murder, Ink (with Gayle Leeson)

Recipes To Die For: A Victoria Square Cookbook

LIFE ON VICTORIA SQUARE

Carving Out A Path

A Basket Full of Bargains

The Broken Teacup

It's Tutu Much

The Reluctant Bride

TALES FROM BLYTHE COVE MANOR

A Dream Weekend

A Final Gift

An Unexpected Visitor

Grape Expectations

Foul Weather Friends

TALES OF TELENIA

(adventure-fantasy)

THRESHOLD

JOURNEY

TREACHERY (2019)

SHORT STORIES

Love & Murder: A Bargain-Priced Collection of Short Stories

Happy Holidays? (A Collection of Christmas Stories)

An Unconditional Love

Love Heals

Blue Christmas

Prisoner of Love

We're So Sorry, Uncle Albert

Writing as L.L. Bartlett

THE JEFF RESNICK MYSTERIES

Murder On The Mind

Dead In Red

Room At The Inn

Cheated By Death

Bound By Suggestion

Dark Waters

Shattered Spirits

JEFF RESNICK'S PERSONAL FILES

Evolution: Jeff Resnick's Backstory

A Jeff Resnick Six Pack

When The Spirit Moves You

Bah! Humbug

Cold Case

Spooked!

Crybaby

Eyewitness

A Part of The Pattern

Abused: A Daughter's Story

Off Script

Writing as Lorna Barrett

THE BOOKTOWN MYSTERIES

Murder Is Binding

Bookmarked For Death

Bookplate Special

Chapter & Hearse

Sentenced To Death

Murder On The Half Shelf

Not The Killing Type

Book Clubbed

A Fatal Chapter

Title Wave

Poisoned Pages

A Killer Edition

WITH THE COZY CHICKS

The Cozy Chicks Kitchen

Tea Time With The Cozy Chicks

www.ingramcontent.com/pod-product-compliance
Lightning Source LLC
Chambersburg PA
CBHW070621170726
48291CB00003B/823